LOYALTY

TAMMY CAPRI

ISBN-13: 978-0615605319
ISBN-10: 0615605311

Printed in USA
Nu Class Publications
PO BOX 23662
Phila. PA 19143

www.nuclasspub.com

DEDICATION

To my motivations: Damien Jr., Dyhmir and Denim, you are truly the reason why I go hard. Mommy loves you! To my #1 supporter, my husband and best friend, Damien Sr. You've been there every step of the way, and I thank you for pushing me to be the best me! To my mom and dad, Cynthia and Stephon, I love you, and thank you for molding me into the woman I am today. Of course, none of this would be possible without my Lord and savior, Jesus Christ. With him, the sky is the limit!

PROLOGUE

June 9, 2010
Dear diary,

Why? Why is this happening to me? It wasn't supposed to be like this. We were supposed to live a long life together, have children and build our home. My baby is gone! I'm going to say my last goodbyes, and if that bitch even show her face at this funeral, I will personally send her to meet her maker!

Loyal closed the diary without reading the rest of the passage. It was the first time she'd opened it since the death of her fiancé, Iras. *This year went by so fast.* Loyal thought to herself as she looked over the obituary of the only true love she had ever known. Emanuel Iras Taylor. April 27th, 1987 to June 3rd, 2010. Stuffing the obituary back into her diary, Loyal could feel the familiar burn of tears pricking the back of her eyes. She hated the reminder of the dark place her mind was in that day, but it was the truth. She was ready and willing to kill for hers.

Loyal placed the diary back into the lock box she stored in her master bedroom's walk- in closet, in a safe disguised as a stack of shoe box. After sealing it shut, she took a few steps to the opposite side and began searching through racks of clothing. With a host of choices and designer labels, Loyal's closet could've easily been mistaken for a high-end fashion boutique.

"Where is it?" She uttered, separating each hanging garment to get a better look. Today, she'd plan to visit Iras' grave site, and wanted to wear his favorite blouse of hers. Even though he was no longer here in the flesh, Loyal still dressed to impress only him.

"Here it is." She snatch the cream, laced, crop top from the hanger, and held it up in front of her to view. For such a simple piece of fabric, Iras loved the top on her. He'd stare at her, and observe the way the soft material clung to her body, hanging just above her navel. Loyal never really understood why he loved it so much, but it was one extra thing she did to make him smile. Iras was her baby. He was the definition of true, unconditional love.

After picking out her attire, she placed it on the king-sized bed and went to check on her little one sleeping in the next room. She had given her nanny, Thelma, the day off. Loyal didn't want any company on this day. This was something she felt she needed to do alone. Standing at the cheery wood crib, she peered over her daughter, Nijah. At only eight-months-old, Nijah had already began taking the features of her father. Loyal wanted nothing more than to have her family complete. She vowed to always keep Iras' memory alive so that her daughter would know the kind of man he was.

• • •

"Thank you, Iras." Loyal said to herself as she looked down at her peaceful sleeping beauty. At that moment, a smile brushed crossed Nijah's face, and Loyal could feel the presence of her deceased love.

"I love you too, Baby!" Tears filled her eye sockets, fogging her vision. After placing a kiss on Nijah's forehead, Loyal headed to the bathroom to shower.

Forty minutes later, both she and Baby Nijah were ready for their trip. It was a first time visit for the both of them. Loyal grabbed the Louis Vuitton baby bag and doubled checked to make sure her black and chrome berretta was still in the secret compartment she had specially made in the lining. Iras taught her well. The life he lived forced her to be prepared for anything and everything. Loyal was his rider, to say the least. Loyal lifted Nijah into her arms and headed down the black wood staircase. The same stairs she vividly remembered him making love to her their first night there. Even after finding Iras dead in their bathroom, moving from their Atlanta home was out of the question. Their last memories were spent within the walls, and that alone was priceless to her.

Loyal walked through the spacious kitchen and through to the two car garage where she kept her black 2011 Acura MDX, with the deep tinted windows and black leather interior. She strapped Nijah into the car seat and then got in the driver's seat. Reaching above her head, Loyal she set the house alarm from the sensor clipped to the sun visor.

"You ready, ma?" She asked her daughter, looking at her through the rearview. Nijah laughed; one of the most pure things Loyal had ever heard. The joy her heart felt anytime Nijah cooed, reminded her how precious life is.

"I will always protect you, baby girl." Loyal said as she slipped the key into the ignition. "Believe that!"

She turned the key.

BOOM!

Monica sat outside in her all white Aston Martin watching the flames consume the house. She anticipated a bigger blast from the one that presented itself. She pulled out her cell phone and hit the send button. The phone rang twice before she heard the silence.

"It's done." She said, knowing her message was heard. She waited a couple of seconds for a response, but only received a disconnected call. Monica closed her phone and drove off. Just thinking about all she'd just gained by eliminating the only person standing in her way gave her an overwhelming happiness. She came, she saw, and she conquered, but at the cost of her own flesh and blood.

CHAPTER ONE
Philadelphia, Pa

One Year Earlier....

Loyal and Melissa pulled up to Climax, an upscale banquet hall located in the heart of Philadelphia. The line to get in was wrapped around the building. It was the night of Iras' twenty-first birthday. After months of planning, Loyal and Iras' father, Eric, were finally able to pull it off. Climax was the place to be tonight. Everybody who was anybody in the city graced the place with their presence. The all black dress code and sixty dollar cover charge kept the crowd at a certain standard. Loyal knew hood rats and bum niggas wouldn't pay that much to party.

The timing was perfect. The famous clique, Young Money, had just finished up a concert a few blocks away. It seemed as if it were just another after party. Iras wouldn't suspect a thing.

Loyal pulled up to the front of the building where the valet awaited her car.

"He is going to be so surprised." Melissa said, looking at all the people waiting to get in. "Do you think he knows about it?"

"Girl, Iras been so busy. A party is the last thing on his mind. He's been so stressed since D-Dos's funeral." Loyal said, turning off her ignition. "Seems like a part of him died that day, too."

"Yeah, they were close as shit, though. You'd think they were brothers instead of cousins." Melissa added.

"I just want to enjoy this night with my baby, and end his birthday the right way—no drama and no bullshit." Loyal said. Quickly checking her lipstick in the visor's mirror, Loyal smiled with approval of her flawless make-up job. "Come on, let's go!"

The ladies walked into the building, bypassing the long line. The party was packed. DJ Breeze had the party rocking. Uncle Luke's, *It's ya Birthday,* had all the women shaking it on the dance floor. Loyal and Melissa headed to the stair case that led up to the VIP section. She spotted Iras' dad and some of his goons popping bottles and entertaining a pack of women; all looking as if they were trying to score a hustla'.

"Here she is. The woman who made all of this possible." Eric said when he spotted Loyal approaching the bodyguard at the VIP entrance. Eric welcomed her with opened arms. "You know what, Miss Loyal? My son is a very lucky man to have you in his life."

Loyal smiled, catching a whiff of alcohol stench seeping from his pores when he leaned in to kiss her forehead. Even through his slight intoxication, Loyal knew he meant every word. Eric always had good things to say about his son's choice. Loyal and Iras had been dating since she was the tender age of fourteen. At that time, Iras was sixteen, but the age difference never seemed to matter. Out of all the girls Iras had in the past, Loyal was the only one he welcomed into her his personal life. She was different. Loyal was smarter than the average teenager. From the day she was old enough to work, she never asked for a hand out. Knowing what she wanted out of life is what Iras admired most about her.

Loyal and Melissa took a seat at one of the high tables close to the railing that over looked the crowd. The waiter came over and took their drink orders. Eric's goons acknowledged Loyal and her friend, and they both could feel the piercing stares from the women they entertained. Barely old enough to be in the club, they had women twice her age envying them.

"All eyes on you tonight, I see." Melissa smirked, nodding her head at the salty-faced pack of women.

Loyal didn't even bother looking. "As long as they don't make me come out of character tonight, I'm good."

Iras' god father, Buttah, walked over and sat his drink on their table. "So where is the man of the night?" He asked Loyal.

"He should be here soon." Loyal shrugged. "Kino said he would have him here by eleven, but you know how that goes."

****

Whack, Whack, Whack!

After a two-hour torture session, Trey's body finally went numb. He barely felt the strikes of the silver chain Kino used to violate his flesh. Trey's scream were no longer audible. His face was swollen, and his cheek bones were completely shattered. Blood continued to drain from the razor tracks Kino engraved into his chest. Even after enduring so much pain, Trey refused to give up his accomplices.

He is one loyal mu'fucka. Kino thought.

Trey was the type of soldier that would have went far on the right team. He was going out like a true *G*.

"This nigga ain't budging, Ras!" Kino said, wiping the sweat beads from his forehead. The weight of the chain he beat Trey with had him exhausted, and his own arm a bit weak.

Kino walked over to his right-hand man, Iras, who was sitting on the pool table in the warehouse rolling a blunt. After lighting one end, Iras took a long pull of the kush, and then passed it to Kino. Iras grabbed the chain from Kino and walked towards Trey's damn near lifeless body.

Hanging by his arms from a thicker chain connected to the ceiling of the warehouse, Trey was dying a slow and painful death; just as Iras planned. He wanted him to feel the same pain that Trey and his homies delivered to his cousin, D-Dos, a few weeks back.

Whack!

Iras whipped Trey across his face with the chain causing his body to tremble.

"Wake up, mu'fucka!"

Whack!

Trey drifted in and out of consciousness. Iras pulled out his 9mm, and pressed the cool metal against Trey's forehead.

Knowing that it was all coming to an end, Trey managed to lift his head so he could stare Iras eye-to-eye. A bloody smirk slowly grew across Trey's face exposing the empty spaces where his perfect white teeth once were. Seeing the tears forming in Iras' eyes was all the joy Trey needed before he died.

"You gon' remember me." He mumbled. "I'm Trey mu'fucka! Laying that nigga down was worth everything y'all tried to break me with!"

The pride of a man on his death bed was a powerful forced. Trey's words strung hard. It was as if Iras' wound were opening all over again.

"See you in hell, pussy!" Trey spat.

"Well when you get there, tell my cousin I sent you!"

POW!

Iras stared at the bloody hole he just put in Trey's forehead. He finally rocked his cousin's murderer to sleep. Iras put a hit out on Trey when he found out about him talking recklessly. He was wearing the murder D-Dos like it was a badge of honor.

Kino paid a stripper to slip a Mickey in Trey's drink one night at a gentleman's club he often visited. When Trey was out cold, the plan went into motion. This was not Iras' first murder. He had been putting in work since he was seventeen-years-old. However, this was the first time it was personal. Killing over money was nothing, but killing for family meant everything.

Iras picked up his cell phone and saw the missed calls from Loyal. He couldn't deal with talking to her at that moment, but made a mental note to call her as soon as possible. He told Loyal everything except for when he laid down a body. He wasn't ready to introduce that side of him. He scrolled down to his father's number and hit SEND. The phone rang twice before going to voicemail. Ending the call, Iras shot him a quick text, knowing that he would see the message sooner or later.

****

The party reached its peak as it approached the midnight hour.

"Where the hell are they?" Loyal hissed after getting Iras' voicemail for the fifth time. "Kino's ass is always late. I knew I should've just drove him here myself."

"He'll be here, L. Here, let me order you another drink." Melissa said flagging over the waiter. Moments later, Loyal saw Eric and his goons rushing out of the VIP, and out of the front door.

From the anger plastered on Eric's face, she knew something wasn't right. Her heart immediately began to beat, nervously. She dialed Iras' number again, and just like the other times, it went straight to his voicemail.

"You cool?" Melissa asked noticing the panicked look on her friend's face.

"Baby, where are you? I'm worried! Please call me back!" Loyal said into the phone before hanging up.

The worse thought cluttered Loyal's mind as she dropped her head into her hands.

"I'm sure Ras is cool." Melissa said, attempting to comfort her girl. "Come on, let's just get out of here."

Loyal downed the rest of her drink before following her friend out of the party.

CHAPTER TWO

"Damn!" Eric yelled, hitting his steering wheel. "What the fuck could've happened?"

He had gotten a text from his son that read, *WH messy. Need to clean up!!!*

Eric knew exactly what that message meant. He owned the warehouse and bought it especially to handle his dirty work. When Iras' turned eighteen, Eric oriented him on how he ran his empire. No, it wasn't to teach him how to kill. The life Eric lived forced him to be open and honest with the ones closest to him. Walking through the street blindly was never an option for his son. If Eric was to get into any bull shit, he didn't want heating coming Iras' way and him not know about it.

Eric was the Tri-State's largest cocaine distributor, supplying the streets of Philadelphia, New Jersey and Delaware. He moved to the next level when he expanded to the DMV area, supplying Maryland, DC and Virginia. Eric even had his hands in a few Burroughs in New York.

Any cocaine that moved was Eric's. On top of that, he owned the largest Real Estate company that sold property out of the top cities across the US including Los Angeles, Houston, Atlanta and Miami.

When they arrived at the warehouse, Eric had two of his men, Stacks and Black, stand guard at the door. Buttah followed closely behind him as they walked into the warehouse where Eric kept several covered cars and an auto lift. To the public's eye, it was just an auto body shop. But a man of Eric's status was well-known in his city.

They walked passed the cars, and to a door with a sign that read *Employees only.* That door led down to the lower level. A dim light softly illuminated the bottom of the dark stairwell, and the smell of Kush filled the air. Eric and Buttah went down and immediately spotted the dead body hanging from the ceiling. Iras and Kino sat atop the pool table in silence.

Eric approached the body trying to make out who it was. However, the person was beaten so badly that his facial features were no longer recognizable. Buttah nodded his head with approval, impressed about the brutal job that was done. That was, no doubt, Buttah's style.

These lil niggas put in some work! Buttah thought. If it wasn't for the ripped jeans and t-shirt dangling off him, the body could've have easily been mistaken for a slab of meat at the butcher's shop.

Eric shot his eyes back at his son. "Ras!" He dominantly called, disappointment lacing his voice. When Iras raised his lowered head and locked eyes with his father's, Eric could see the emotion built up in them. "Let's go."

Eric walked passed the guys, and headed back up the stairs.

Iras could tell his father wasn't too pleased with what he just witnessed. After giving both Kino and Buttah fist bumps, Iras spoke. "I'll come pick my car up from your crib in the morning." He told Kino before heading up the steps.

"Alright bro!" Kino replied.

Eric walked out the warehouse passing Stacks and Black. "Clean the mess up down stairs." He ordered before getting into his car.

Iras emerged from the building a few moments later. He walked passed the men without acknowledging either one of them, and climbed into the passenger side of his dad's Benz.

The ride to Iras' place was silent. Eric thought about all that he had been through to get to claim his current position. He looked over at his son, who seemed to be consumed by his own thoughts. Iras was the splitting image of his dad. Eric couldn't help but chuckle when he noticed how close the resemblance was at that very moment. It was as if he was looking into the past, and saw himself at that age. Iras was hard-headed to say the least. Just like his father, he always had to find out things the hard way. Eric pulled up to the luxury condominiums where both Iras and Loyal lived.

"I don't want you to think I'm trying to run your life." Eric started, breaking there forty minute silence. "I just want you to think about the decisions you make. That *shoot first and ask questions later* mentality you have is what's going to be the death of you one day. I know there had to have been a good enough reason for things to play out the way they did, but shit, it's other ways you're supposed to handle it. Whatever beef you got out here, you bring it to me. You got your whole life ahead of you; you don't need to be getting caught up in this shit. I was lucky enough to get passed it, now I got niggas to handle my dirty work. This life is temporary, and you're going to find out sooner rather than later making messy ass moves like you did tonight."

Iras stared out the window as his dad tried to school him. All he could think about was his cousin, and how he found him in pieces inside one of their trap houses in West Philly.

"I bought you into this to show you how to make this bread without having to do it the way I did." Eric continued. "All of this is going to be yours one day. Why do you think I'm turning everything into a legit business? I'm doing this so you won't have to." Eric took a deep breath. "Iras, I need you to promise me that you're going to keep your hands clean from now on."

Iras wondered why his father never asked his motives behind it all. He wanted to tell his dad that D-Dos died at the hands of the man hanging back at the warehouse, but his father always told him that a man with excuses have no confidence in his decision. Excuses are the tools of the incompetent.

"Son, I love you. If anything ever happened to you, I don't know what I would do."

"I know pops." Iras said in a low tone. "I will fall back... I promise." Iras got out the car and shut the door.

Eric pressed a button on the middle panel and slid down the passenger side window. "Yo Ras!"

Iras turned around. "Yeah, dad?"

"Happy Birthday." Eric said before pulling off.

Iras nodded his head. Even though it may seem as if Eric's words went in one ear and out the other, Iras felt where his dad was coming from.

Loyal sat on the couch drinking a glass of Red Irish Rose. When she heard a car door slam shut, she jumped up from her seat and looked out the window. Relieved, she let out a deep breath when she saw Iras walking up to the entrance of their building. Loyal sat back down on the cozy sectional and turned off the television moments before Iras walked in. Emotions were running high, and tears began to take form in Loyal's eyes.

"Do you have any idea how worried I was?" She fussed the second Iras walked through the door. "Dammit Ras! Why weren't you answering my calls? All types of crazy shit was running through my mind when—" Loyal stopped mid-sentence as Iras stepped closer to her. The distraught look on his face turned her frustration into concern. His eyes were red and puffy as if he was the one crying all night.

"I'm going to take a shower." He told her.

Loyal could feel his troubled vibe, and at the point decided to drop the issue. Whatever happened tonight had him at an all-time low. Her man needed his woman, and as usual, she was going to be there for him.

Iras stood under the running water wishing it would rinse away the hurt he was feeling. The warm water hitting his body like little massage beads felt perfect; just what he needed after a crazy ass night. Loyal walked into the bathroom and slipped out of her white silk robe, revealing her nude body. She opened the shower door and stepped in behind him. Wrapping her small arms around his mid-section, she held him tightly, pressing her body against his. Her five foot, five inch petite frame fit perfectly up against his six foot one inch muscular build. Both caramel complexions, their bodies melted together as one. He rubbed her hands, embracing the cradle she offered. Her tight grip spoke volume, letting Iras know she'd walk through his pain with him.

A mixture of tears and water flowed down his cheeks. Losing his cousin still felt like one big nightmare. It was a harsh reality he was forced to live each day.

"I love you, baby." Loyal whispered.

Iras turned around and lifted her up into his are. Her legs locked around his waist. He kissed her, passionately, while turning to put her body under the water.

Loyal's love-box began pulsating, starting the ignition of her grinding hips against his mid-section.

Iras' kisses moved down to her neck causing her juices to flow. He wrapped one of his arms around her back and slid his other hand down her front side, massaging her clit.

Loyal closed her eyes, and enjoyed all of it.

Iras carried Loyal out of the shower and into the master bedroom, never taking his lips off of her. Not caring that both bodies were dripping wet, he laid her down on the king-size bed.

Loyal grabbed her perky breast and gently caressed her hardened nipples as Iras made his way down to her sweet pearl, leaving a trail of kisses along the way.

He circled his tongue around the lips her of pussy, zoning in on her clit. He could tell by the squirming of her hips that it drove her wild. Loyal grabbed his head pushing his face deeper into her. He sucked on her clit causing her lips to release a soft a moan. He loved tasting her, and she had no complaints.

Iras stood up, massaging his manhood. He sat on the bed next to her, and pulled her on top of him. As she slid down onto his rock hard dick, his shaft disappeared inside of her, making him weak. Digging his head back into the pillow, Iras close his eyes and held on for the ride. Loyal rode him like a pro. Her juices cover his stick and dripping down to his sac.

He grabbed her breast and fondled her nipples, knowing how much that turned her one. In full ecstasy, Loyal began bouncing on his dick, faster and faster. Her pussy took the wheel and pressed the gas pedal for full speed. The vibrating feeling from her trembles had Iras stiff. Their breathing got heavier and heavier, leading up to the sound of pleasure they both released after reaching their climax. He let off everything inside of her, and her pussy swallowed all of it. Loyal collapsed on his sweaty chest and noticed how his heart beat matched hers, perfectly. That confirmed it for her; they were meant to be together.

"Happy birthday, baby." She said.

But Iras had already drifted off to sleep. She laid there alongside of his body and eventually joined him.

CHAPTER THREE

Monica sat a few doors down from Eric's house in a black tinted SUV. She had been watching his house every night for the past week, hoping that Iras would visit his father. After waiting almost two hours, she saw a navy blue Lexus jeep pull into Eric's driveway. Monica sat up in her seat, and anxiety kicked in when she saw Iras step out of the driver's side. Even though it was the first time she laid eyes on her son since he was younger, she knew exactly who he was. Her first instinct was to run to him, but she felt paralyzed. She watched as he walked around to the other side of the car and opened the door. A woman stepped out, and he escorted her into the house.

Emotions filled Monica's body. She put her hand on the window, wanting so badly to touch him. Retrieving an ink pen from her bag on the next seat, Monica wrote his license plate number on the back of her hand. Moments later, Iras and his lady friend walked back outside.

Monica's mood quickly turned to rage when she saw Eric step out behind them, escorting a dark skinned woman. They all piled into Iras' car and backed out of the driveway.

When they were far enough away, Monica started her engine and followed them. Keeping her distance, she made sure she didn't blow her cover. After the twenty minute drive, they finally pulled up to Castello's Italian Restaurant. Monica watched as the group entered the upscale establishment. She hated Eric with a passion. The man she once loved turned into the man she hated with every cell in her body. Seeing Eric and Iras together took her mind back to the time when she and Eric first met.

Summer of 1987

"Mo, if you play this song one more damn time, you gon' be walking to the movies." Angel said jokingly.

"You need to stop worrying about me and pay attention to the road." Monica said, dancing to her favorite song in the passenger seat. "I would like to live to see eighteen."

Angel had to laugh at her best friend's response. Both of them knew that Angel had about as much driving skills that a white girl had rhythm. She managed to steal her father's car for their night on the town. It wasn't the first time she'd taken it out for a joy ride without him knowing. She would snatch his keys to make a quick mall run, or grab something from the market, and would return the car back to its place, unscratched. But the ladies made plans that would have them out all night. Angel knew she was treading shallow water, but she needed this night out with her friend. It was the only normalcy she had to escape her crazy life.

"You sure your daddy won't find out about this?" Monica asked, feeling a bit skeptical.

"Trust me. My sperm donor is laid up somewhere with one of his hoes. I'm the last thing on his mind. He probably won't be home until sometime in the morning."

"But this car is too fly." Monica said, admiring the decked out red leather interior. "If he isn't checking on *you*, I know he'll be checking on *this*."

Angel's father, Mac, drove a red Nissan 300ZX convertible. It had gold rims to match the gold trimming around the base of the car. Mac was once one of the most respected men in Philadelphia. He was a pimp with a tight murder game. Mac feared nothing and took no bullshit from anyone. When Angel was born, he had no idea that he even had daughter. Her mother, Daisy, was an escort that worked for him. She was one of the best in the game. She only dealt with business men that came into Philly on business trips, paying top dollar for her services. Her small belly made it easy to keep her pregnancy a secret the entire time. At seven months, Mac was arrested on a petty charge and spent five months behind bars. It was perfect timing. Daisy hadn't even come up with a game plan to give birth without Mac knowing, so a huge weight was lift from her shoulders.

The only person who knew about the baby was Angel's grandmother, PearlyMae. When Angel was about seven-months-old, Daisy got hooked to the popular drug, cocaine. Needless to say her top dollar pussy turned into a stray kitty cat. She wasn't bringing in the money she used to, and Mac had already found her replacement.

The day before Angel's first birthday, Mac beat Daisy half to death for trying to rob him. He left her to die in an alleyway in West Philadelphia. Her body was found two days later by a homeless man.

PearlyMae took care of Angel for the next twelve years. Angel heard many stories about Daisy, and how beautiful she was. She inherited her soft chocolate complexion, big eyes, and high cheek bones from Daisy. PearlyMae told her about times she had to sleep in the room with Daisy when she was a younger because of her fear of the dark; Angel picked that up as well. PearlyMae shared it all, and to Angel, Daisy seemed like the perfect woman. However, when Angel would ask how her mother died, PearlyMae had a way of avoiding the question. She knew the truth would tarnish who she created Daisy to be in her child's eyes. Truth was, Daisy was nothing but a rebellious, troubled child, who grew up to be an even worse adult. Nonetheless, PearlyMae did tell her that maybe one day she'd meet her father, yet praying Angel never had to.

One day when Angel came home from school, she'd found her grandmother lying in the bed. PearlyMae looked as though she was sleeping, but when Angel tried to wake her, PearlyMae didn't respond. Angel laid next to her grandmother and said a prayer before calling the ambulance. That was the last day of her normal life. Angel had no clue of who her father was, but birth records helped Social Services track him down, and she was sent to live with him in southwest Philadelphia shortly after.

At first, Mac didn't want her. Providing care for one of the many children he helped conceived was the farthest thing from his mind. If it weren't for her strong resemblance between them, he would have denied her completely. She had his thick lips and flat forehead. But the more he stared at her, the more he could see her mother. Dollar signs filled his eyes, and his old habits resurfaced. Even though she was only a preteen, Angel was already coming into her womanly physique. She was about 5'6, 119 pounds. With her coco brown complexion and hazel eyes, Mac definitely saw her potential. Angel was beautiful but needed work. A skinny little girl who rocked a ponytail and a baseball cap, her innocence was pure.

It didn't take long for Mac to rip her purity out of her like a gutted fish. Angel's innocent was taken on her thirteenth birthday when Mac put on her on first job. Angel had her first Ménage à trois experience with a young couple looking to have a good time. They did everything you could possibly imagine to her. She made her first hundred dollars that night. After that, Angel was hooked.

Angel attended Shaw middle school where she and Monica met. Monica was the only one who knew her money making secret. The both of them have been like white on rice ever since. They went to the same high school and shared clothing— Monica even did little side jobs with Angel from time to time.

One night they made, seven hundred dollars by having a three some with one of the high school teachers. To them, they were set. They could buy anything they wanted, and they did.

One a regular day, they were laced with the latest trends and rocked fly hairstyles. They were the finest girls at Overbrook High School. By the time Angel was fifteen, she had more sexual experience than someone twice her age. By senior year, she went from scrawny to *God Damn*. Monica was also eye candy.

She was 5'7, light brown skin, and thick in all the right places. She rocked a short hair style with honey brown highlights. Her perky breast added two years to her age, and her plump ass sealed deals. Her curves had grown men begging like little boys. They had *it,* and definitely knew how to work it.

"Damn, the line is long as shit!" Monica complained as they pulled up to Capitol Theater.

"Line? What line?" Angel had no intentions on waiting in line like a homeless person at a shelter. She never did, and never had to. Scanning the crowd, Angel smiled when she spotted the perfect prey. Two geeky looking boys stood three spots away from the front.

"Bingo." Angel nodded. "Hey you!" She yelled to the boys. One of them, along with some other people, looked her way. The boy pointed at himself with his eyebrows raised in disbelief that a beautiful girl would be calling him out of all people.

"Yea you," Angel waved for him to come over. The boy looked over at his friend, who was also shocked by the breath-taking females.

"Close your mouth man. I'll be right back." He said before walking toward Angel's car.

"What's up?" Angel asked him as he approached.

"Do I know you?" He replied, hesitantly.

"The question is do you want to know me?" Angel said, offering a seductive look.

"Oh, I di-di-didn't know i-if you were c-c-calling me o-or not."

A stutter? Ain't that a bitch? Angel thought as she held in her laugh. "Yea, I was. Me and my home girl were checking y'all out. What movie are y'all seeing tonight?"

"We're a-a-about to sss-see that nnn-new movie T-Top Gun."

"Word! That's what we were going to go see! Mind if we join y'all?"

A huge grin spread across the boy's face at the thought of him being so close. The excitement obviously traveled down to his manhood because Angel could see a small bulge growing in his pants.

Monica discreetly shook her head looking over at her friend. *Her ass ain't no good.* She chuckled.

"Look," Angel said as she started to caress the boy's hand. "Why don't y'all get our tickets, and we will get the popcorn."

The boy looked down at Angel's very exposed cleavage through her low cut black tank top. His dick was now at full attention.

"No, ma. yyy-you don't have ttt-to get anything. This nnn-night's on us." The boy ran back to his friend waiting in line.

"I-I know y-y-you don't expect me to be s-s-seen walking in there w-with them bizarre looking n-niggas." Monica mocked, laughing hysterically.

"Bitch, the moment we get in, we're ditching those lames." Angel said fixing her makeup in the rearview.

A few minutes later, the boy returned to the car. This time, with his friend.

"Y'all ready?" He asked, handing Angel two movie passes. "This is m-my boy BBB-Benny, and I'm J-Jamal."

Benny need to miss a few meals! Angel thought as her eye shifted to the large framed guy. "Hi, Benny. I'm tiny, and this is my home girl Phat Phat; and yes we are ready!"

Benny and Jamal walked behind Monica and Angel as they entered the theater.

"Jamal, we're going to go to the ladies room before the movie starts. Can you find us some good seats? We like to sit on the balcony." Angel reached up to him, gently tracing his earlobe.

"Ok, no problem." Benny and Jamal headed towards the balcony stairs. As soon as they were out of sight, Angel and Monica walked into the lower level of the theater, making sure to sit under the balcony so they would be spotted. The place was jammed pack with movie goers. Rows and rows of people from couples and families to groups of friends, the girls were lucky to find two empty seats in the row next to the last.

Halfway through the movie, Monica got up to use the bathroom. Angel had fallen asleep and she didn't even bother to wake her to let her know. Monica walked towards the ladies room.

Shit. Why this fat ass nigga thinking about food and the movie is almost over? She thought when she spotted Benny waiting in the concession line. She hurried into the restroom without him seeing her. Two woman were heading out just as she had entered. Monica quickly glanced around the well-lit, three stall ladies room before entering the first stall.

After relieving herself, Monica flushed the toilet, washed her hands, and checked herself in the mirror making sure her makeup was still intact before heading out.

"I hope his fat ass isn't still out here." She uttered.

When pulled on the think door, a tall light skin guy with braids stood there blocking her in.

"Excuse me," she said, sucking her teeth.

"He's not gone yet, but I can move if you want him to see you." The guy replied with a smirk. "So, do you ladies do that all the time?"

"Do what?" Monica spat. "And I believe I said *excuse me.*"

"Do you always use your looks to get what you want?" The guy continued on as if not to notice Monica's apparent attitude.

"I don't know what you're referring to, but for the last time, EXCUSE ME!"

The guy stepped to the side and let her out of the restroom.

"Ain't nobody even out here." Monica said as looked around the lobby.

"I'm out here." He smiled.

Monica looked up at him and before cursing him out for briefly holding her hostage, she couldn't help but notice how handsome he was. He had a light faded beard and dimples. He wore an all-black Adidas baseball cap, and a black and white Adidas warm up with all white Adidas shell toe sneakers.

Monica ogled him from head to toe, and could tell he wasn't one of those lame, broke niggas.

"I peeped what you and ya home girl did to ole' boy." He laughed, shaking his head. "Y'all know that wasn't even right. Sending those boys home, heartbroken."

"I didn't do anything but accept a gift." Monica folded her arms across her chest. "We offered to buy our own, but they insisted. So…"

"So what? You out here gold diggin'?"

"Nigga, please!" Monica put her hand on her hips and shifted her weight to one leg. "So do you do *this* all the time?"

The guy turned his head and chuckled, exposing a tattoo on his neck of three dollar signs. He couldn't help but laugh at her attempt to be so hard and look so good at the same time.

"Do what?" He asked.

"Do you always stand at bathroom doors, wait for women to come out who you've been spying on all damn night, and chastise them?"

"No, but I couldn't help myself when I saw you."

Growing annoyed, Monica turned on her heels and began walking away. "You on some creep shit dude." She mumbled.

"Creep?" He followed behind her. "I'm far from a creep. I just know what I like. I was gonna get at you when you first got out of the car, but I didn't want to throw salt on y'all game. When I saw you going into the bathroom, I figured this was my chance. Sorry if I came off wrong. I just wanted you to know that I think you're beautiful."

Monica stopped in her tracks and turned back towards him. "Thank you..."

"Eric." He said. "My name is Eric."

"Well, Eric. I appreciate the compliment, but you need to work on your approach." She briefly looked away and then back at him. "I'm Monica. And I am far from anybody's damn gold digger. I get my own shit, believe that!"

"I didn't mean it like that, ma."

"Um-hmm," Monica offered. "Look, I need to get back in there before my home girl send out the state troopers. Thanks for the small talk... Maybe I'll see you around."

"I hope so, Miss Monica," Eric said as he watched her walk back into the theater. Even though she seemed a bit younger, there was something about Monica that had him wanting to know more. He was surely going to find out.

It was a little after 1:30 AM when the movie ended. Monica was ready to call it a night.

"I feel like getting a drink. Can we hit up one of those after hour spots?" Angel asked her friend as they headed towards the main exit.

"I bet you do. Your ass slept through the damn movie." Monica said jokingly.

When they reached outside, it look as if it were a club let out. People lingered around the sidewalks, cars were double parked in the streets, and as usually, they were loud as they wanted to be. Monica and Angel walked through the crowd ignoring all the lame niggas who tried to run game, and crossed the street to where they were parked.

"I don't understand dudes these days." Angel shook her head. "Knowing damn well they got girlfriends sitting at home waiting—"

Pop Pop!

Loud gun shots alarmed the crowd causing everyone to scatter in every direction.

"Oh shit!" Monica screamed as she and Angel hurried into the car and pulled off.

"Move!" Angel yelled trying to maneuver through the crowd.

Monica spotted Eric and another guy running down the street. "Wait, slow down." Monica said, never taking her eyes off of Eric.

"Bitch, what? Niggas is out here trying to murder somebody and you want to—"

"Just slow down."

Angel huffed and pressed on the brake pedal.

"Need a ride?" Monica shouted out as the car slowed down. Without saying a word, Eric and his friend jumped in the backseat of the convertible. Angel pulled off and turned the corner. A few more gunshots rang out off before the sound faded.

"Thanks, ma." Eric sighed in relief.

"Don't mention it," Monica responded. "I'm guessing you didn't run to the movies theater tonight. Where's your car, or are you a passenger seat rider?"

"My car was parked around the corner where the shooting started. We had to make moves in another direction." Eric said. "But I see you're very comfortable in the passenger seat."

Monica had to laugh at how dumb she sounded for trying to play him out and she wasn't pushing her own set of wheels.

"Umm, who the hell are they?" Angel asked irritated by the way her friend just invited two strangers in the car.

"An old friend," Monica answered while looking at Eric through the rearview mirror.

"Well, *old friend*, where are you getting out at because this damn sure ain't no taxi cab." Angel hissed.

"You can let us out up here at the corner," Eric said pulling a knot of money from his pocket. He peeled off two one hundred dollar bills and a card and passed them both to Monica. Angel pulled the car over letting the guys out.

"Thanks for the ride, ma. That should cover your gas." Eric said to Angel pointing to the crisp bills he gave to Monica. Eric looked at Monica and smiled before Angel pulled off.

"Mo, what the hell was that about?"

"I think I just made me a new friend," Monica smiled. She folded the money and put it in Angel's ash tray. Monica began to read the business card he passed to her.

ABM
EMONEY 215-555-2343."

"Yea, a new friend..." she repeat to herself and tucked the card in her pocket.

Honk, Honk!

A car honking nearby broke Monica out of her trance. She scanned the restaurant through the window and spotted Iras and his party sitting in a booth. She picked up her cell phone, dialed a number and hit the speaker button.

"Hey Beautiful!" A man answered.

"Hey, baby. Where are you?" Monica asked.

"I'm just getting to work. Why, you stopping by for a midnight treat?"

"Anything for you, baby." Monica licked her lips. "And I need a favor."

Chief DiLucci Come in!

Monica could hear the dispatch through the phone.

"Hold on, beautiful." He told Monica before putting her on mute.

Silence filled the line, momentarily. Monica glanced back at her son. They joy spread across her face made her heart thump faster. "I'm here, baby." She whispered. "Mama is here now."

"Sorry about that, sweetie." The guy said, returning to the line. "Now, what's this favor you need?"

"I need you to look up an address for me; I have the license plate number." Monica said. "I want to surprise an old friend of mines who I haven't seen in years."

"And what do I get in return?"

"Joe, baby, you know I got you. Same time, same place right?" Monica said in a seductive voice.

"My cock is getting hard just thinking about it." Joe moaned.

Monica wasn't never really into white men, but Joe had two things she needed—money and power. Both were required if she'd ever wanted to get back into her son's life. Joe DiLucci was Philadelphia's Chief of Police. Monica met him shortly before completing here drug rehabilitation program. Joe had been there a couple of times for different workshops about law enforcement. Even he couldn't believe a woman so beautiful was caught up in drug addiction.

It was true what people say; the higher the position, the grimier the game. Two weeks after she left the program, Joe spotted her waiting at a bus stop and offered her a ride. His intention was to taste a piece of her sweet candy. For as long as Joe had been in the field, he was certain Monica would relapse like the rest of the drug addicts. Their payment to him for keeping them out of jail was any sexual favor he desired. He was ready to add Monica to his list. He wanted her since the first day he saw her in rehab. But little did he know, Monica had intentions of her own and captured the one thing he had trouble controlling—his heart. Ever since then, Monica used him as a pawn in her game.

"Thank you, baby. I'll get the address from you tonight." Monica said before ending the call.

A devious grin laced her face as she pulled out of the parking spot. "We will meet again very soon, my son."

CHAPTER FOUR

"So that's the plan, huh?" Teresa asked Angel, with a heavy Latino accent, as she sat up on the side of her bunk.

Angel laid on her back staring up at the chipped paint on the jail cell's ceiling.

"Hell yeah, girl. One thing for certain and two things for sure, I'm in no rush to be back behind these walls." Angel said.

"I feel you, girl." Teresa nodded as her eyes scanned over a paper she held.

The two had been cellmates for a little over two years. It was Teresa's first institution; however Angel had been to several over the last two decades. At first, Angel never acknowledged her presence. Teresa was the new girl, and Angel was set in her ways. Their age gap played a part in it as well. Teresa was young and dumb. Angel could tell by the way she talked so loosely about her sentencing.

Teresa took the life of a girl at a bar over a spilled drink. She had the game twisted. Inmates could care less about what you did to get there; it was about surviving once you got there.

Angel knew to keep her distance because all of the bragging Teresa did could only mean two things—Teresa probably couldn't back up any of the tough talk, or she was the type to sing like a blue bird to the guards.

It wasn't until one day another inmate tried to get Teresa to take Angel out. Angel was well- known and well-respected, but with respect came haters and envy. There wasn't many who had the heart to even attempt to handle Angel themselves. Those who did ended up hanging by their ankles with a slit throat, or drowned in a shit-filled toilet bowel.

Teresa knew there was a reason why they wanted her to do it, and as soon as she found out Angel's status, she murdered the inmate who made the offer, hoping that would prove her loyalty to Angel. If she was going to be down for somebody, might as well be someone with clout. When Angel got word of what she did, she saw a different side of Teresa. From then on, Angel took her under her wing and showed her the ropes.

"Angel?"

"Yeah what's up?" Angel replied.

"All this time we've been cellmates, you never told me your story?" Teresa said.

"My story?" Angel looked over at her cell mate with puzzled eyes.

Teresa scooted to the edge of the bed. "Yeah, your story? How did you end up here in the first place?"

Angel chuckled and turned her head back towards the ceiling. "Oh, I murdered someone."

Teresa wasn't satisfied with her answer. She stood up and walked over to Angel's bed.

"You know my story, right?"

Angel laughed. "Who *don't* know your story?"

"So tell me yours." Teresa pushed Angel's legs over, clearing a spot for her to sit. "What happened, because you definitely don't seem like the street type. I mean, in here you got people to handle shit for you. You're smart. I see that. But I can also see through you. This little role you're playing up in here ain't fooling me."

"Alright." Angel sat up with a serious look on her face.

"You want to know my story? I'll tell you my story. You know the feeling you get when you want the person who hurt you to feel every bit of pain you felt?" Angel started.

Teresa nodded her head.

"Well, that was when I know I had it in me..."

Summer of 1987

It was a little after two a.m. when Angel pulled up to her house after taking Monica home. She noticed that the lights were still off, and the windows were closed.

"Glad his ass isn't home because I don't feel like his shit tonight." Angel said, parking her father's car two spots down from where it originally was. Hopefully he wouldn't notice it was even moved. She took the two crisp one hundred dollar bills from the ash tray, slipped them into her bra and made sure the car was secured before heading up the front steps. Angel unlocked the front door, and entered into the dark living room. Her heart skipped a beat when she saw the orange glow from the tip of the lit cigarette.

"Where you been?" A man asked her from across the room.

Angel didn't need light to see know who it was. "Mac, I didn't think you were here." She said, nervously. She had always called her father by his name. "I went to see Monica for a little while and lost track of time."

"Any clientele tonight?" Mac asked as he turned the lamp on that sat on the side table. Wearing only a pair of boxer shorts, Mac sat on the single chair with his feet resting on the ottoman.

"Look, Mac, my friend really needed me tonight. She was going through something and she needed me. I got some things lined up for tomorrow; I promise I'll make it up then." Angel tried to remain calm so she wouldn't seem as though she was lying.

Mac slowly stood up and put his cigarette out on the table. He walked over to Angel and stood in front of her. Angel could smell the stench of liquor, and the moment he invaded her personal space she knew something was about to happen. She just prayed that it would be quick tonight.

"Let me get this straight, you were out all night, stole my car, *and* you didn't make any money?"

"Mac, I said I will make it up tomorrow." Angel said, trying not to make eye contact.

"I think now is a good time to make it up." Mac raised his hand up to her breast. With his eyes trained on her daughter, he began teasing her nipple with his thumb.

Angel's body tightened up. She closed her eyes as tears burned through her lashes.

Mac used his free hand to grab hold of the other nipple. When Angel felt his lip on her neck, she backed up.

Mac glared at her with threatening eyes. "What the fuck I tell you about resisting? You are my property. I can do whatever I want to you. Move again, and I'll make sure that pussy bleeds this time."

Without saying a word, Angel squeezed her lids tighter. Her chest heaved up and down as she felt Mac's hands positioning around her waist. Roughly, he backed her up to the door.

"Mac, please don't do this." Angel pleaded as more tears broke loose from her eyes.

Ignoring her request, Mac proceeded to rip her tank top and exposed her black laced bra. His five foot eleven, 310 pound stature was too much for Angel to fight him back. The last time she tried, he pistol whipped her until she fell unconscious. She even tried running away but was spotted by one of Mac's homies when she got to the Greyhound station. That stunt earned her an ass whooping and a baby. Mac was so high he didn't bother pulling out. Carrying a baby implanted by her father was enough fuel to end her life. Before she even realized she was pregnant, her body miscarried.

Dying seemed much more calming then the hell she was living in. She came to the suicide rode a few times but never had the heart to complete the task. Angel learned a long time ago not to piss Mac off, and she kept it all a secret. She never even told Monica about the abuse from her father.

Mac pulled out one of her breast and bent over to suck on her brown nipple. When he noticed money falling to the floor, he instantly stopped. "What the fuck is that?"

Angel heard the change of tone in his voice and was afraid to ask what he was talking about. She looked down to the floor and saw the bills lying by her foot.

Shit! She thought. That quickly, she had forgotten about the money she had tucked in her bra. Angel looked at Mac without responding.

Smack!

The force of Mac's hand against Angel's face left a burning sensation on her skin. Angel grabbed her cheek as Mac struck her over and over again causing her to fall to the floor.

"You think you can steal from me too, huh bitch?" Mac said as he continued to pound his fist into her body.

Angel curled up into a fetal position trying to keep her head safe from his blows. Mac beat her until he was tired. Luckily for Angel, that wasn't too long after.

Mac had been drinking that night, and the intoxication had him winded. Huffing and puffing, he stood straight up, towering over his daughter. He wiped the sweat dripping from his forehead with his hand and walked back to the chair he was sitting in.

"If you ever steal from me again that will be your last day breathing." Mac threatened as he sat down in the chair and lit his cigarette.

Angel lifted her head to see where he was. She felt like she had just been hit by a truck. Her cheek was slightly swollen from the smack across her face.

Mac finished his cigarette never taking his eyes off of her. "Crawl your ass over here and apologize the right way." He demanded.

Angel knew exactly what he was talking about. She hesitated.

"Don't make me have to tell you again." Mac said in a lower tone.

Angel crawled slowly over to Mac. She pulled out his already hard dick and began to stroke it with her hands. Mac put his head back and slouched into a more comfortable position. He watched as she put her mouth on the tip of his penis and began sucking on the head.

"That's right," Mac moaned and grabbed the back of her head pushing her further down his shaft.

A fresh set of tears flooded her face. Angel hated Mac with a passion. She tried to think of the times when she was most happy. When she was with her grandmother, her life was good. Mac was a black shadow casted and rain fire on her life since the day she met him.

She knew that if she stayed there he would eventually kill her. Leaving was not an option for her either. Angel had to make a more permanent decision; one that she didn't have to look over her shoulder the rest of her life.

As her eyes rolled up to look at him, her heart turned black. It was as if the devil took over her body. She no longer felt guilt or remorse. Her conscience was nonexistent, and her mind was made up.

She was going to end Mac's life…

One week later

"Are you sure this is safe?" Peaches asked Mac as she applied her makeup in the compact mirror. "We never came this far out for a job."

"Bitch, would I be here if it wasn't safe?" Mac replied. "This is one of my VIP customers paying top dollar. You better act like you know." He shook his head at the thought of his ladies questioning him. His first instinct was to smack her but he knew VIP clients wouldn't pay for a bruised bitch. A bruise on any hoe makes them look like a street worker. Mac was about his money, but later he was going to make sure she remembered who was running the show.

Peaches opened her purse and pulled out a small plastic baggie with four blue pills.

Mac noticed her intentions and quickly snatched the bag from her. "Didn't you hear what I said? This mutha'fucka is paying top dollar! Top ma'funckin dollar! You're not about to fuck this up for me by being zoned out."

"But Mac, I need them to do every job. I be all nervous and shit." Peaches said folding her arms and sat back in the seat.

Mac ignored her argument and pulled into a parking garage at Whitehouse Suites. It was the most expensive hotel on the forty minutes outside of the city. Mac pulled out his phone and dialed a number. A woman answered on the first ring.

"416 right?" Mac confirmed.

"You're late." The woman spoke.

"I know," Mac said. "But I have something to make up for it."

"Hurry up." the woman hissed and then ended the call.

Mac cut his eye over at Peaches giving her one last look-over. "Let's go."

Peaches looked around at the fancy manicured landscaping. She never had a problem with fitting in with the wealthy.

Even though she barely had two nickels to rub together, Peaches always looked and acted the part. She'd only been working for Mac for about six months. Mac used her for the big jobs. Everyone in Philly thought she was his new girlfriend instead of a worker. Peaches wasn't the corner type, and at times Mac wore her on his arm like a trophy. This was her third job, but the first time she expected to actually have sex. Before this, she was only used twice to satisfy a politician and his crazy fetishes, and to her surprise, sex wasn't involved. Peaches and Mac walked into the front entrance of the hotel. The lobby had a water fountain carved into the letters WH with soft lighting coming from the bottom of the shallow pool. Mac led her to the elevators and proceeded to the 4th floor.

"This hotel is fly, how come we never came here?" Peaches said, admiring the layout in the elevator. Mirrors covered the elevator walls, and a gold chandelier hung from the ceiling.

Mac shook his head and smiled. He used to think about just making her his lady, but his trust in woman was very slim. Mac never knew his mother, and was nearly killed by a woman after she set him up when he tried his luck in the drug game. From that point on, women only had one use to him, even his own daughter.

Peaches was the only type of woman he could see himself with if he ever decided to settle down. She was beautiful and a bit rough around the edges, but she demeaned attention everywhere she went. She took care of the womanly duties in Mac's life, and no matter how much he threaten to hit her, he never really did.

When they stepped off the elevator, Mac walked toward room 416. Peaches followed behind him discreetly checking the wire she had taped to her chest.

She had been undercover trying to catch her big fish, but never had enough evidence to reel him in. Tonight, she knew she had him. The door was cracked open when they approached. Mac tapped the back of his pants reassuring himself of the 9mm he had on him. He pushed the door open and slowly entered the suite.

Immediately, he spotted the burning candles giving off the aroma in the room, and a bottle of Champaign chilling in an ice bucket next to it. On the table in front of the couch was a card with a lipstick kiss print and it read: *Send her to the bed, take a seat and enjoy the show!*

Mac's eyebrows rose the same time as his dick. "Oh, I forgot to mention. This client is a woman." Mac said with a smirk on his face as he sat on the couch full of red and white rose pedals, which also led a trail to the bedroom.

"Well, money is money!" Peaches said as she closed the door and locked it. "I'm going to go freshen up before she gets here." She kissed Mac on his neck and massaged his rock hard dick, teasing him before she disappeared into the bed room. Peaches walked passed the king size bed and toward the bathroom. She walked in and locked the door behind her.

"So what's the plan?" Peaches asked as she hopped up on the bathroom counter. The shower door opened and Angel stepped out of her hiding space wearing an all-black Chanel leather one piece, black knee boots and a long black wig with a bang cut just above her eyes. She walked over to the mirror and began applying her makeup.

"We kill 'em!" Angel said never taking her eyes off the mirror.

Peaches was caught off guard by her response. Angel asked her to help set Mac up to be robbed and thought she could eventually use this set up to use against Angel to finally catch her prey.

But when she heard the word *kill*, she knew shit was about to get deep, fast. She didn't want to blow her cover but at the same time, she couldn't let a man die, and especially not under her watch. Peaches' heart began to pound in her chest. She didn't know what she was going to do, but she knew she had to do something.

"Kill him?" Peaches asked with furrowed brows.

Angel smirked at the look on Peaches' face. Angel had every intention on killing her too right after she did Mac. There wasn't anything personal, but after being raised by scum she picked up on certain rules. Catching a body was a one man secret. Keeping Peaches alive would sooner or later risk her freedom. Trust no man, or in this case, a bitch. Period.

"Listen, you just get him settled and I'll handle the rest. When I'm done, you take your money and disappear, got it?" Angel said as she checked out her back side in the mirror. She never looked Peaches' way.

"I got it..." Peaches said before walking towards the door. "Just wait for my signal. Wait until you hear music playing."

Peaches left the bathroom and headed back to the living room. She noticed Mac had made his way to the balcony.

"A girl could get used to this," she said admiring the view as she stepped closely behind him. The hotel featured a huge swimming pool with lights at the bottom that changed colors. The water fall and cave added the final touches. "I feel like I'm in the Bahamas or some shit."

"Well, don't get use to a damn thing." Mac said. "This is business." He turned to enter the suite, smacking Peaches on her butt as he passed by.

"Oh, we're going to need ice. The ice machine is at the other end of the hall." Mac picked up the ice bucket and held it out to her.

Peaches looked at Mac through the side of her eye and shook her head. She took the bucket and walked toward the door not saying a word.

Mac got even more aroused watching her walk away from behind. Peaches wore a black backless halter dress with a low V cut that hugged her body just right. Mac had no complaints as he watched her walk out the door. He poured himself a glass of Champaign and walked through the propped open French cut double doors that separated the living room from the bedroom. He sat his glass down on the glass shelf next to the entertainment center. He picked up the remote and turned on the radio. Smooth sounds of Luther Vandross filled the air. He sat on the bed, took his jacket off and laid it next to him. Mac laid back on the bed and closed his eyes, grooving to Luther.

Angel heard the music playing and pulled out a 38 caliber hand gun. "It's show time." She whispered as she slowly opened the door. She could see Mac lying on the bed. She crept as close as she could get without him grabbing her. Angel aimed the gun directly at Mac's head. She wanted to hurry up and get it over with but not before hearing him beg for his life.

"Bitch ass nigga!" Angel said, getting Mac's attention.

Mac opened his eyes and quickly sat up when he saw a woman standing there threatening to take his life.

"Move and I will blow your fucking brains across the room." Angel said.

At first, Mac hadn't recognized her; but after hearing her voice he knew exactly who she was. "Angel, what the hell are you doing?"

"Shut the fuck up! I'm running this show!" Angel cocked the gun back and aimed it back at her father. Mac wanted to reach for his pistol, but after looking into Angel's blank stare, he knew she was serious. It was as if she was lifeless, no soul. He knew she was ready to kill.

"I don't know if you're crazy or just fucking stupid, but whatever it is you need to come to your senses quick!" Mac demanded, trying to put the fear back in her. "You hear me, bitch?"

"SHUT THE FUCK UP!" Angel released a bullet from the chamber, hitting Mac in the shoulder. "Next time it's going to your dick! You do what I say!"

Mac grabbed his bleeding shoulder and cringed to the bed.

Peaches dropped the ice bucket when she heard the gun go off. She pulled out her pistol from under her dress and ran down the hall to the room she had just left out of. She stood on the side of the door and cocked her gun back.

Mac knew he had to do something because his chances of living were slim at that point.

"I hope you know you're dead! If I live to see another day just know you signed your own death certificate."

Angel fired another shot this time hitting him right above the genital area. Mac fell to the floor in the worst pain he'd ever felt. "YOU FUCKING BITCH!"

Angel shook her head at how much pride he had. Even as he faced his expiration date, he still felt no remorse for his wrong doings.

"I must not have made myself clear. Now, you got one chance to confess your sins and maybe, just maybe, God will spare your life."

Mac couldn't respond. His breathing got heavier as his vision got blurry.

Peaches got low and slowly turned the door knob. She could hear Angel talking and what seemed to be grunts from Mac as she entered the room. She spotted Angel standing over Mac's bloody body ready to finish what she started.

"Angel, drop your weapon. Think about what you're doing." She pleaded trying to stall time. Angel was so zoned out she didn't even realize Peaches was standing there. Mac sighed in relief when he saw Peaches. Relief turned to confusion when he heard the next words coming out of her mouth.

"Officer Fisher needing back up and an ambulance, I have a ..."

Pop Pop Pop!

Angel sent three bullets right into Peaches' chest. Peaches dropped to the floor making a loud thump. She turned the gun back to Mac and put another bullet into his neck before making her exit.

"Ahhh, Fuck!" Mac screamed. He looked across the room at Peaches struggle for air. Building up enough strength, Mac slid over to her. He didn't want to believe that he let a cop into his circle. He pulled the top of her dress down revealing the mini microphone. The rage that overcame him was unbearable. He put his elbow on her neck and pressed with all his weight, blocking what little air that kept her hanging on. Peaches grabbed him but wasn't strong enough to fight back. When he saw the life leave her body, he rolled over and gave into the sleepy feeling that he himself was fighting.

Angel ran down the hotel stairwell to the third floor where she had purchased a room earlier that day. She quickly removed her disguise and put all her belongings into a back pack. She put on a pink T-shirt, a pair of cut off denim shorts and tennis shoes.

"Shit!" She huffed. "What did I just do?"

In a frantic panic, she began pacing the floor trying to figure out her next move. Before she could even replay the entire ordeal in her mind, flashing red and blue lights hit against the balcony's sliding glass door.

Angel rushed over to the balcony and looked down. Police cars were everywhere. Her heart thumped loudly in her ears. *I gotta get out of here!* Angel thought, hurrying over to the bed. She grabbed her backpack, rushed out the room, and jabbed at the elevator button.

Be cool, Angel. She coached herself as she stepped onto the empty elevator. The ride down to the lobby seemed as though it was taking forever. Butterflies swarmed her stomach, and her legs were starting to go numb. *You're almost out of here, be cool.*

When the doors opened at the lobby, she saw nothing but black and blue uniforms. One cop approached her as she was getting off the elevator. Angel's heart beat sped up with each step he took to close their gap.

"Excuse me, Miss." The cop called. His eyes scanned her from head to toe. "I'm sorry, but I have to keep this area clear."

Angel smiled at the officer. "I just need to check-out. I have a flight to catch in an hour and I'm already running behind."

"Again I'm sorry, but you're going to have to wait a while." The cop said looking back at his sergeant. "At least until my boss goes upstairs." The cop gave Angel a wink and smiled, exposing his dimples.

Angel smiled back and nodded.

Ding!

The elevator door next to them opened up, and EMTs came out pushing a stretcher that carried a body covered with a white sheet. Angel knew by the small frame that it was Peaches.

"You probably shouldn't see this. It may give you nightmares." The cop said to Angel, using that as an excuse to touch her. Placing his hand at the small of her back, he guided her a few feet away from the elevator.

"What happened to her?" Angel asked with her eyes trained on the stretcher. She tried to keep the conversation going long enough to catch a glimpse of Mac's dead body.

"How do you know it's a female?" The cop said in a joking manner. His question broke Angel's attention from the paramedics leaving out of the hotel.

"Huh? Oh, um… well you know, I figured it was because the person looks tiny." Angel explained. *I need to get the fuck out of here before I say the wrong shit.*

Ding! Seconds later, the elevator door she'd just stepped off of opened up. When she turned around to look, her heart dropped to the floor. I was indeed the person she wanted to see, but knew for sure he's be covered as well.

Mac laid on the stretcher and the paramedics pushed him out of the elevator. He was covered in blood, and wore an oxygen mask on his face. Mac was still conscious, but barely. Clinging on for dear life, his eyes locked with his daughter's. It was as if they both were looking in a mirror. At the exact moment, their evil's matched. It was the day Angel's life changed, yet again.

CHAPTER FIVE

"Oh shit!" Teresa was shocked, jaw wide open. "So, he wasn't dead?"

"Nope," Angel shook her head. "I mean, he died later that night in the hospital. But he was able to tell them who his attacker was. They even tried to pin Peaches' murder on me too."

"How the hell you manage to death row?"

"The only thing that saved me was the mark on her neck where he suffocated her. My lawyer came to the conclusion that he was the one who finished the job by the trail of blood Mac left when he slid across the floor. She could have survived, but she was suffocated. I took the plea bargain for murder two and got twenty to life."

"Damn…" Teresa said taking in all in.

The cell grew quite as Angel started to think about how long she had been locked up. Twenty-three years, four months, two weeks, five days, and eight hours. Her first week behind bar, she knew for sure she wouldn't survive her first year in prison. Her days were long and tired. Her hope decreased with each failed appeal attempt to lesson her sentence. Like any mammal in a habitat, Angel adapted and made the best of her new home.

"Angel?" Teresa called.

"Yea?"

"I got a letter from mi' madre', and she was letting me know about my kid brother."

"Oh yeah, how's he doing?" Angel asked. Teresa talked about her brother so much Angel felt as if she knew him, personally. Angel knew she loved her brother a lot, and secretly she wished that she had someone in her life that she could connect with the way they did.

"He's missing." Teresa told her as the tears began to form in her eyes. "My mama said he'd been missing for about a week."

Angel could hear the hurt in Teresa's voice as she tried to play it cool. The news was killing her.

"She said he went to a gentleman's club one night and wasn't heard from since. He was all she had left. I've failed her; I won't be getting out of here any time soon. I'm spending the rest of my life in this place and now my kid brother is missing." Tears started to flow down Teresa's cheeks as she thought about how her life had completely changed.

Angel sat up in her bed. That helpless feeling Teresa was experiencing was one that Angel knew all too well. Many nights were spent trying to rid herself from that feeling.

"Can you do me a favor?" Teresa asked.

"Anything."

"We're from the same city…you and me."

"Yea, I know." Angel said, waiting for Teresa to continue.

"Well, when you leave here tomorrow, please try and find out what happened to him. And write me to let me know if he's dead."

"Say no more. I'll find out." Angel said before pausing. "And if he's dead, I will personally lay to rest the person responsible."

Teresa looked up at Angel and could see the seriousness in her face. "You don't have to do—"

"Teresa, you're like a sister to me. And I owe you my life. You could have taken me out a long time ago, but you chose not to. What you did back then put you on a lot of people's shit list. But I respect that. And for that, I will do this for you."

"Angel, you don't need to do anything that is gonna get your ass sent right back here."

"Trust me, when I leave, I'm not coming back." Angel assured. "Don't worry about me."

Teresa got up and hugged Angel, tightly. She then walked back to her bed and took the picture of her brother Emilio off the wall. It was the most recent photo she had of him. Angel gazed at the photo. He was the splitting image of Teresa. The back of the picture read *Emilio Jose' Santos III aka Trey.*

"I'll find out what happen to him," Angel nodded, eyes glued to the photo. "You have my word."

CHAPTER SIX

Loyal stood at the kitchen counter chopping up onions and green peppers. Iras' birthday week was coming to an end and she was preparing a romantic dinner for him. Loyal had the music blasting as she danced around the kitchen reciting the words to Meek Mills new joint *Make Em' Say*. After a long night out on the piers of Atlantic City, New Jersey, Loyal was beat. Iras was already up and out the house, and would be gone all day handling business in DC, which gave her time to prepare his dinner surprise.

Loyal saw her cell phone light up and Melissa's name flashed on the screen. She turned the down music and answered.

"Hey Girl!"

"Hey, what's up with you? We still on for today?" Melissa asked.

Loyal had asked Melissa to go shopping with her. She wanted to buy a new outfit for this evening.

"Yea, we're good." Loyal replied. "Let me just hop in the shower and get ready."

Ding Dong!

"Who the hell is at my door eleven o'clock in the morning?" Loyal asked out loud.

"Alright well, go answer that and I'll be there soon." Melissa told her.

"Alright girl." Loyal ended the call as she walked to the front door. She looked through the peep hole and saw a woman standing there holding three gift boxes. Loyal disengaged the alarm and unlocked the door leaving the chain connected.

"May I help you?" Loyal asked the women through the cracked open door.

"Hi, I'm sorry to bother you, but I'm looking for Emanuel." The woman answered.

She must be a cop, Loyal thought. Only certain people knew that Iras was not his first name.

"I'm sorry but you've got the wrong address." Loyal said.

"Are you sure? Emanuel Taylor?" The woman asked trying to read Loyal. She could tell she was lying.

"Yes, I'm sure! No one by that name lives here." Loyal said shutting the door.

The woman put her foot in the doorway, stopping it from closing. "Look, I'm just trying to reach him. When you see him please give him this." The woman pulled out a folded piece of paper and passed it to Loyal through the door. She put the gifts down on the ground and headed out of the building.

Loyal closed the door and ran to the window. She watched as the woman climbed into a black SUV. Curiosity started to sink in because Loyal had never seen the woman before.

She walked back to the front door and opened it to retrieve the gifts. Her first instinct was to open them, but didn't want to hear Iras' mouth. *Maybe Iras knows who she is,* Loyal thought. She placed the gifts on the coffee table and didn't think any more of it. She showered, dressed and waited for Melissa to arrive.

Monica got back into her truck and pulled off. "Who the hell does she think she is lying to me like that?" she hissed to herself. "I should have kicked that fucking door in on that little bitch!"

She was just being safe, it's not her fault. Monica thought.

She battled with voices in her head ever since she stopped doing drugs.

"Safe my ass! And what do you know?" She asked herself looking in the rearview mirror. "She knows who I am. She's just trying keep me from my son. They all are."

You're right. So, get rid of her.

Get rid of her? She didn't nothing wrong.

It's the only way of getting your son back.

"Shut up!" Monica yelled as she pulled up to a stop sign. Yelling at herself was one way she controlled her schizophrenic diagnosis. Monica put her head down on the steering wheel and took a deep breath, trying to regain composure.

Beep! Beep!

The car behind her pulled up along the side of her truck. "It's a stop sign, lady. Not a red light!" A fat white man shouted.

Monica peered up at the car as it got in front of her. The expression on her face turned cold. Her mind was playing tricks on her because what she saw was the girl that just answered the door at her son's place driving away in the car, and she convinced herself that it was leading her to her son.

She followed the car for about fifteen minutes before it pulled into a mini mart parking lot. Monica pulled behind the car blocking it in the parallel parking space. She hopped out of her truck not even bothering to turn off the ignition. As she approached the car, her mind made her see the girl talking on a cell phone. Monica opened the door and grabbed the girl by her neck. She violently shook her, attempting to squeeze the life out of her.

"You little bitch!" Monica shouted as she began to pound on the girl. "You know who Emanuel is!" Monica beat the girl until she was unconscious, letting out all of her frustration. She looked around, breathing heavily, to see if anyone was watching. The parking lot was empty, but when she looked back down, she saw what was really going on. The fat white man was slouched over and covered in blood.

Monica's eye bulged out of its sockets as she covered her shocked open mouth with both hands. Stunned by what she just did, she slowly backed out of the car and stumbled back to her truck. Her hands trembled like little vibrators covered in blood. She didn't know if the man was dead or not, but she wasn't going to stick around to find out.

In a hurry, Monica left out of the parking lot trying to get as far away as possible. She drove until she reached the suburbs of Philadelphia, where the more expensive houses were. She pulled into a gated community where each house had a manicured lawn, and curbside mailboxes. Being there made her feel as if she wasn't in Philadelphia in anymore. The streets were clean. Even the air smelled fresher. When she reached her destination, she pulled her truck in front of the two car garage, turned off the ignition, and pulled out a compact mirror. Her face was a sweaty mess. Between the dried up tears, and specks of blood that splattered on her face when she beat a man half to death, she was in no shape to be seen by anyone.

"Pull yourself together. It was an accident." Monica told herself as she reached for the wet-naps from her glove compartment and scrubbed the blood off of her hands and face. She scrubbed so hard that her skin complexion changed to a light tint of red. Monica pulled a cigarette out of her purse and lit it. She sat back in her seat trying to calm herself.

All she could think about was how good it felt when she thought she was beating the shit out of that girl. Monica's heart grew cold over the years. She learned a long time ago that this world that she lived in did no favors for her. Everyone she'd ever cared about was either taken from her or dead. She was left alone in the jungle to survive without protection. Her only *friend* that seemed to help her cope through it all was a white powder treat that consumed her life.

Just thinking about it made her body tingle. She took another drag of her cigarette when she heard someone calling her name. She looked up and saw Joe standing at his front door, waiving for her to come in. Monica put out her cigarette and stuffed the bloody wet naps under her seat before following his direction.

*****

Loyal and Melissa were out shopping for the past three hours. They were in and out of damn near all the stores in the shopping mall. During her outing, Loyal copped two outfits, one for the main course and one for desert, including a pair of cherry flavored edible underwear. She wanted this night to be perfect. It was after 4 pm when they arrived back at Loyal's condo.

"Ugh. I didn't expect to be gone so long." Loyal complained. "Ras is going to be home soon and I still got a lot of shit to do."

"Why are you tripping? Romance is my specialty." Melissa said flopping on to the couch. Loyal gave her the side eye knowing her girlfriend was full of shit. Romance was the last thing on her mind when it came to men. That bitch was about her money. She had the mentality of most niggas. *Fuck em' and duck em'.*

"Nah, leave the romancing to me, but you could finish cooking for me, though." Loyal said with the sad face. Melissa could cook her ass off.

"Well, let's get to it." Melissa said.

Three hours passed and the condo had transformed into her personal love nest. Scented candles were place everywhere, red rose littered the floor, and dim lights made the room feel extra sexy with the candle. Loyal set up a table in the living room made for two, and had two bottles of Moet on chill in the ice bucket. All that was missing was a server, but Loyal had plans to wait on her man hand and foot.

"Okay boo, my time is up." Melissa said walking into the bedroom.

Loyal had just finished showering. She sat at her vanity wearing only a white plush towel. She looked at her friend and smiled. "Thanks Liss. You are a life saver, Cherry flavor!"

"Yeah, I know." Melissa said jokingly, but meant it. "Have fun, and I want details in the A.M. I'll lock the door behind me on the way out."

"Bye, honey." Loyal said as she applied her make up. Loyal picked up the phone and dialed Iras' number.

"Hey, beautiful." Iras answered.

"Hey, baby. Where you at?"

"I'm on my way to you; just got off the highway, about to drop Kino off."

"Ok well, I'll see you soon then."

"Alright."

Loyal hung up the phone, and slipped into a white Gucci dress with a gold chain belt that draped from her waist and gold open toe stilettos.

The dress left nothing to the imagination. She walked into the living room and turned on the stereo. Smooth sounds of Jagged Edge filled the air.

Soon after, Loyal heard a car door shut and she peeked out of the window. She spotted Iras walking up to the building, carrying two black duffel bags. As Iras entered the building, Loyal noticed the lights on another vehicle come on and the vehicle pulled off. Her hood instincts started to kick in when she noticed that it was the same truck she had saw the lady who was there earlier get into. Loyal didn't want to ruin the night by bringing it up to Iras, but she made a mental note to make him aware first thing in the morning.

Iras walked in to Loyal standing in the middle of the living room floor holding two glasses of Moet, and wearing more skin than clothes. He admired her perfect physique in her tight fitted navy blue dress. Slowly, Loyal spun around to show off her attire. Iras walked to her and grabbed her by the waistline.

"What's all this?" He whispered in her ear.

"The perfect ending to a perfect birthday for the perfect man." Loyal said, grinning from ear to ear. She wrapped her arms around his neck. "Everything is for you, baby."

"Everything?" Iras asked as his hands made their way down to her plumped assets.

Loyal moaned as she kissed her man passionately. "Come have a seat right here." She said leading him to the table in the living room.

"One second. I need to make a deposit first." Iras said, referring to the money he made on his trip. He kept his stash in a safe in the master bedroom.

"Don't keep me waiting." Loyal demanded.

Iras smacked her ass before picking up the duffel bags and heading to the room. He went directly to the closet and opened the door to a rack of clothing.

After pulling out several suits and laid them on the bed, Iras pushed the rest of the hanging clothes to one end of the closet exposing a locked compartment in the rear. He unlocked the latch and opened the door to get to the safe. Entry to the secured box required three different combinations. It was one of his best investments he'd ever made, and only three other people knew of the safe spot. Iras put thirty thousand and ten bricks of cocaine into the safe and sealed it shut. After closing the closet, he noticed gifts on the bed. Being the nosey person he is, he opened the largest gift box first. It contained an all-white Armani three piece suit and diamond cuff links. He admired the suit and loved the fact that his lady knew his taste. He closed the box and opened another one while listening out for Loyal. He didn't want her to catch him in the act. The second box he opened caught him off guard. The first thing he saw was a picture of a beautiful woman holding an infant. The baby looked to be a couple of days old. The box was full of pictures. He picked up another photo of the same woman but this time she was holding an older baby.

Iras was confused. He wasn't sure why Loyal would give him a gift of old photos. He was about to close the box when he spotted another photo. This time it was a picture of the woman, his father and a little boy. At that moment, he realized that the little boy was him. He had never seen that woman before. He picked up the box and headed back to the living room.

"Where did you get these pictures from?" Iras asked as he walked towards Loyal.

"What pictures?" Loyal asked, sensing his mood change.

"From the gift… where did you find these photos?" Iras asked again sitting the box on the table where she was sitting.

Loyal was clueless as to what he was talking about. She picked up one of the pictures from the box and immediately noticed the woman in the picture. "That's her!" Loyal said.

"Her who?"

"That's the woman that came by here today."

"Woman? What woman?" Iras asked, even more confused than before.

"Some woman came by here for you earlier today." Loyal explained. "I didn't want to mention it just yet because I didn't want to fuck up our night."

"Wait, what?" Iras started, "Some random woman comes by here looking for me, leaves gifts, and you didn't call me?"

"Babe, she asked for you by Emanuel. I didn't know who she was."

"All the more reason why you should have hit my jack. For all I know she's the fucking Feds or some shit."

"Look, I told her she had the wrong house. And if she were, I doubt we would be standing here talking right now because the same car she got in earlier today just pulled off when you came in." Loyal blurted out. She didn't mean to be so loose with her words, but it slipped out.

Iras looked at Loyal trying to figure out what tip she was on. She was never the type to allow some suspicious shit go on and not tell him.

"So I'm being watched now, too?" Iras asked pacing back and forth in the living room. He didn't know what was going on.

Loyal sighed, deeply. "Ras, can you please just clam down. Everything is going to be fine." Loyal began looking through all of the photos. "Oh my God, baby, is this woman your mother?" She asked in shocked.

The same thing that already crossed his mind also came to hers.

"My mother is dead, and you know that. For her to be my mother, that would mean that my father lied. It would mean that he kept this from me my entire. My father don't lie."

Loyal walked over to him and handed him a picture. It was the woman holding little Iras next to a Christmas tree. "I think you need to call her." Loyal said in a low tone. She retrieved the piece of paper from the TV stand that the woman left with her number on it.

Iras took the number and walked back into the bed room. Anger grew as he began to accept the fact that his father may have kept this from him all this time.

Loyal sat back on the couch looking through more photos. She couldn't believe that the woman who stood in front of her earlier that day could really be Iras' mother. She came across this one photo that was taken in the hospital. Eric was holding a new born baby. He seemed so happy. His smile was as big as someone who had just won the lottery. Loyal sat the picture aside and put the rest of the pictures back in the box.

"I'll be back." Iras said walking back into the living room.

Loyal stood up and followed behind him. "Where are you going?"

"I'll be back!" He repeated with annoyance lacing his tone.

Startled, Loyal didn't say another word as she watched him walk out of the door, slamming it behind him. She didn't know if he was more upset with her for not telling him about the visit, or at the fact his father could be lying to him about his mother. Whatever it was, she knew not to push the issue. Loyal couldn't help but feel as if this was all her fault.

Why didn't I just call him? She thought, blaming herself for the ruined evening. Loyal poured herself another drink and sat down on the couch trying to wrap her head around all that was happening. She picked up the picture of young Iras and the woman. She even started to see the resemblance.

A few hour had passed as she waited up for Iras to return. It was after 1 A.M when exhaustion kicked in. Finally, she retired to the bedroom, alone.

CHAPTER SEVEN

Iras and Kino were at the Gentlemen's club damn near all night. After receiving such a crazy gift, he called his boy to clear his head. He told Kino what went down.

The news shocked him as well.

"I know your pops," Kino said. "That nigga is one straight up dude. That bitch got to be lying."

"Pictures don't lie, man. I know it was me in the pictures." Iras explained as he took a drag of the Kush Kino rolled up for him. It was approaching the 5 a.m. hour and there were only about ten people in the joint. Iras wasn't a big fan of strip clubs. Pussy was Kino's drug of choice. It had been ever since they were teenagers. Iras always said Pussy was going to be the death of Kino one day.

"I still think the bitch is lying." Kino repeated as he took a sip of his drink.

"Yo, that nigga ain't God. Stop sitting up here acting like he can't do no wrong," Iras snapped back.

"So now you refer to yo' pops as nigga?" Kino shook his head. He knew it had to be the liquor talking.

"If the shoe fits! My whole life he been telling me stories about my moms, how he wished she was here to see me now; giving me the bullshit. He knew all this time. He would say, 'a real man don't lie, a real man owns up to his mistakes." Iras said as he picked up his drink. "We gon' see how much of a real man he is." Iras took the last sip of his drink and slammed the glass down on the table. "Yo, order me another drink, I got to take a piss." He told Kino as he got up from the booth and headed to the bathroom.

Kino didn't respond. He had his eye on one of the strippers, Meeka, getting ready to leave out. She was new to the club, but Kino had already found out about her from one of the other girls. Kino got up from the booth and caught her before she reached the door.

"Leaving so soon?" He asked her.

Meeka ignored him and kept walking.

"Excuse me!" Kino called out.

Meeka stopped in her tracks and looked over her shoulder at him. "I don't do personal jobs okay."

"Good, because neither do I." Kino shot back. That statement flowed out his mouth too easily— as if it were true. He had a piece of just about every girl that worked there.

"I just wanted to introduce myself, ya know? On some gentlemen shit."

"Gentlemen shit, huh? In a pussy bar? I don't think so." She said, proceeding to the exit.

Kino rush in front of her, stopping her yet again. "Would a gentlemen offer to walk you to your car? It's definitely not the right time of morning for a beautiful woman to be walking alone." He said, extending out his hand. "I'm Kino."

"I don't drive, Kino. My ride is waiting for me. But thanks anyway." Meeka said, sarcastically.

They both approached the exit door. Kino held it open as she walked out. A black Impala sat idling along the curbside. The letters DT were made into the rims. Meeka walked directly to the car and got in.

Kino tried to see who was inside, but the door opened and closed to fast. Kino stepped outside and lit a cigarette not wanting to make it obvious that he was scoping shit out.

The car pulled off, and Kino took a glimpse of the license plate. It read *IAMDT*. Kino threw out the cigarette and went back inside the club to get Iras.

Where the hell have I seen that car? He thought. Kino did so much dirt in the streets, he was always aware of his surroundings, especially faces. He knew Karma would catch up to him eventually, but he wasn't about to make it easy for the bitch.

Iras was sitting back at their booth when Kino walked in. Old timers, Lexi and Miss Gage, were in the sixty-nine position teasing whoever was still watching. Iras was so consumed with his thoughts that he wasn't paying either one of them any attention.

Kino tapped Iras on the shoulder. "I'm about to be out my nigga, you good?"

"Yeah I'm good." Iras replied. "I'm going to chill here for a little bit, though."

"Are you sure?" Kino said knowing his friend wasn't in any condition to be alone, even worse drive.

Iras nodded his head as he sipped on his drink.

"Alright then, hit my jack when you get in the crib."

The men bumped fists, and then Kino headed out of the club. Iras wasn't ready to really be around Loyal, or anyone else for that matter. Even though he knew she meant well, his stubbornness wouldn't let him stop being mad at her. All he wanted right now was answers, and only two people had them. He pulled out the piece of paper with Monica's number on it. He pulled out his cell phone and dialed her number. He hesitated before hitting the send button because it was so early in the morning, but it was something he had to do.

"Yea, is this Monica?" He said when the groggy-voice woman answered. "It's Emmanuel. I got a message you were looking for me…"

CHAPTER EIGHT

Angel sat in the parole office waiting for her meeting. She had been there almost an hour and still hadn't been seen. She looked around noticing how different things were. She had been away from the world so long, time had passed her. A young guy sitting across from her kept adjusting the cuff at the bottom of one of his pant legs; seven times in the last five minutes. Angel knew he was trying to hide that tracking bracelet and could tell he was nervous. Her lockdown intuition started to kick in and she grasped the razor blade that she kept in her pocket. A person acting funny in the pin normally means someone was about to get it, and it wasn't going to be her.

The guy noticed her grilling him, but she didn't care. Her hard exterior is one of the reasons she made it out alive. The tension grew weird and uncomfortable, eventually causing the guy to get up and walk to the restroom. Angel kept her eyes on him as he walked to the back.

There is definitely something up with that kid, she thought.

"Caldwell!" Angel heard her last name being called. She got up and walked over to the cubical where her parole officer was stationed. A fat white man sat at the desk typing on the computer. He never took his eyes away from the screen. He gestured for her to sit in the chair across from him.

The smell of sour cream and cigarettes blew passed Angel's nose.

"Where is Mr. Jacobs?" Angel asked, referring to her parole officer. Angel had never seen this guy before.

The man ignored her question and handed her a urine cup. "Fill this up." He demanded. His tone made Angel's blood boil. She could tell he was an asshole. The kind of man who think his authority was equivalent to God. There were too many guards like him in prison.

Snatching the cup from his hand, Angel looked him dead on letting him know she don't take no bullshit. It wasn't much she could say to him without messing up her situation, but she was going to get her point across one way or another.

"Leave it in the sink." The man said as he rolled his eyes and turned back to his computer.

Ten minutes later, Angel returned to the cubical. Before she even had a chance to sit down, gun shots sounded throughout the office. Chaos broke loose and everyone tried to run for safety. Angel dove under the desk. More gun shoots sounded over screams and cries.

"Everyone stay where you are!" A woman shouted. A few more shots fired before it all finally ended.

Angel could hear the police sirens getting closer. She crawled from under the desk and saw the fat white guy covered in blood. He was gripping his neck with both hands gasping for air.

"Oh shit! This man was shot!" She yelled.

Three officers rushed over to the cubical pushing passed her. One officer asked her to step out and take a seat back in the waiting area. Angel followed his order. When she stepped out, she saw that nervous-looking kid she grilled down earlier. He was laid stretched out on the ground dead and a semi-automatic laid not too far away from him. Angel shook her head.

I wonder what made him snap. She thought.

It had to be deep for him to pop a PO. From what she could see, only three people got hit: the kid, a cop and the fat white guy from her meeting. Paramedics and police officers filled the building. A security guard stood at the exit door letting people out. Angel walked out and headed straight to the car. She had only been out of prison a week and already the craziness was starting. She decided to cancel the rest of her plans and head back to the house to regain composure.

Angel stayed with Teresa's uncle, Pablo, in North Jersey. Teresa put Pablo down on what Angel was doing for her. Pablo immediately gained a respect for Angel. He set her up in one of his safe houses. Teresa had already told her how powerful her uncle was. His pull was stronger than a magnet. Angel didn't mind, in fact, she felt safer knowing she was in the hands of such a powerful person.

He gave her a key to the house and loaned her a car so she could get around. He said she could stay for as long as she needed to, but her plans were to get her own spot as soon as she got on her feet.

As far as her task, she had no leads on Trey's disappearance. She had already come to the conclusion that he was dead, but she felt the need to at least find the person responsible. The only thing was that the streets were so quiet you could hear a pin drop. Getting any type of information was harder than she thought.

Angel pulled up to the house and parked on the street. She was greeted by an empty house as usual. She barley seen Pablo, but he would call her from time to time to check on her. From what Teresa told her, he spent most of his time out of the state. She didn't know exactly what he did, but judging by his spare house, he was paid. She could only imagine what his real house looked like.

The only other person who knew of the house was his daughter. She was in college and would often stay there when she was home for breaks. Angel never met her, she was supposed to come home for the summer but Pablo said she was staying with her mom in Puerto Rico.

Angel went upstairs and ran herself a bubble bath. She went into the front room and turned on the light. She took off her clothes and wrapped a towel around her dark tone body. She tied her hair up and laid back on the bed waiting for the tub to fill up.

Ring! Ring! Ring!

Pablo's land line sounded throughout the house. It was the first time she had ever heard that phone ring. All incoming calls for her came through her cell phone. She sat up in the bed and looked at the phone. She decided not to answer it, knowing it wasn't for her anyway. Ignoring the ringing, Angel went to enjoy her bath. After unwrapping the towel, she let it drop to the floor and stepped into the Jacuzzi tub. The space was big enough to fit at least eight additional people. She slid her entire body from the neck down into the water and turned on the jets. Moments later, the phone rang again. The ringing continued for about two minutes before stopping.

Angel closed her eyes and relaxed her body. Ever since she got out of prison, bubble baths were her therapy. She knew how shitty it was showering in lock up, so she made sure she enjoyed this luxury.

The phone started ringing once again. Her plans to ignore it went out the window when the person wouldn't stop calling. Angel got out of the tub, picked up her towel and wrapped it around her body. She walked into the hallway where the cordless phone was sitting on top of a table. Just as she approached the phone, the ringing stopped. She looked at the caller ID which read *Unknown Caller*.

The phone rang again with the same unknown caller ID. Angel pushed the table over to get to the phone jack. The handset fell from the base and on to the floor.

"Hello? Pablo!" She heard a woman say from the other end.

Fuck! Angel thought. She didn't expect for the phone to pick up. She quickly pressed the end button and unplugged the phone jack. She went back into the bathroom and got back into the tub. The hot water and bubbles against her skin was the soothing she needed after such a long day. She thought she would never take another bubble bath. Angel had been locked up since she was eighteen years old. She thought about how different her life would have been if she hadn't taken her father's life.

Her thoughts took her all the way back to her grandmother, and how her life had changed the day Mac polluted it. A single tear slid down her cheek. It hurt her to think that her grandmother knew of all her wrong doings. Even though she'd been dead for many years, she could feel her grandmother's heart breaking at the sight of her only granddaughter. Angel had no other family left. The only person she considered family was her best friend, Monica.

Monica kept in touch with her for almost a year after she went to jail, but just like everything else in her life, the letters and visit died out. Angel tried reaching out to Monica here and there over time, but never got a response.

Feeling relaxed, Angel started to drift off to sleep.

Boom, Boom, Boom!

"What the—" the noise startled her. Someone was banging on the front door like they were the police. Angel got out of the tub and wrapped her towel around her to go see who was at the front door. Surprisingly, she didn't make it that far. When she opened the bathroom door, three automatic weapons were pointed at her.

CHAPTER NINE

"Ha! Taste this!" Iras said holding out the spoon for Monica's approval. She took a small bite of the roasted chicken he prepared.

"Not bad." She said nodding her head and taking another bite.

"I told you. I don't play in the kitchen."

"Well, you must get that from me because from what I can remember your father couldn't cook a hot dog." Monica said, grabbing two plates from the cabinet.

"Monica?"

"Yeah?"

"Where were you? I mean, why did you wait all this time to come back?"

Iras' question hit Monica like a dagger. It was a question she knew he would eventually ask, but she never prepared the answer.

Monica stopped what she was doing and turned to look at him. "Emanuel, life has a way of moving on its own even if you don't go willingly. I'm not the same person I used to be. I've made some bad decisions that took away my options. When your father took—"

Ring! Ring!

Iras looked at his cell phone and saw Loyal's picture pop up on the screen. He sent her call to voicemail. It took him weeks to build up the courage to have this conversation with Monica, and he didn't want any interruptions.

"Go on," He told her. "My father took what?"

****

Loyal was greeted by Iras' voicemail, again. As much as she didn't want to believe that he was stepping out on her, the signs pointed in that direction. Over the past couple of weeks, she noticed a change in him. Iras spent more time out, and checked in less. Most of the time she didn't know where he was. Loyal opened her cell phone and dialed Kino's number hoping that Iras was with him.

"Yo?"

"Hey Kino, what's good? Ya boy with you?" She asked, trying to remain cool.

"Nope, ain't seen that nigga in a couple of days. Is everything ok?"

"Yeah, everything's cool. I think his phone is dead, and I was just checking on him." She lied.

"Cool, well if I hear from him I'll tell him to hit you up."

"Thanks, Kino."

"One." He said before hanging up.

Loyal closed her phone and placed it back into her hand bag.

"You okay?" Jackie asked after noticing the expression change on Loyal's face.

"Yeah, I'm cool." Loyal said.

Jackie was Loyal's hair stylist. She has been keeping her fly for years and Loyal knew better than to tell her business in the shop. Jackie's mouth was looser than a hoe's ass.

Loyal pulled out her cell phone again and called Iras. She grew anxious as she heard each ring, waiting for him to pick up. Still, there was no answer. Her intuition ate away at her gut like as if it was the last supper.

How did I let another bitch slide into my spot? She thought. She wanted answers, and was going to get them by any means necessary. Loyal ended the call and dialed Melissa's number. She was going to need help if she wanted to get to the bottom of it all.

CHAPTER TEN

Angel threw her hands up and her towel dropped to the floor exposing her naked body. One of the men pushed his way into the bathroom and ordered the other two men to finish searching the house. Angel picked up the towel and covered herself. She didn't know what was happening, but she prepared for her death. The other men came back to confirm that the house was empty. The guy took out his cell phone without taking his eyes off of Angel. He briefly spoke in Spanish to someone on the other end before gripping her by the arm and leading her down stairs to the living room. The other two men followed with their guns blazing, ready to pop off at any sudden movements.

What shit is this Mutha fucka into? She thought. She looked around trying to plan a getaway but they would most likely shoot her before she reached the outside.

Angel knew her death would be a harsh one because Karma was a big bitch you didn't want to fuck with, but she at least wanted to go out for something she did. She didn't know what was going down.

The front door opened and in walked a young woman with long black hair. Angel instantly recognized her from the photos around the house. She was Pablo's daughter. The guy that held Angel spoke to the young woman in Spanish as she walked closer.

"Who are you, and how did you get in here?" She asked Angel.

All Angel could do was focus on the guns pointed at her waiting for a bullet to leave the chamber.

"I needed a place to stay and Pablo was generous enough to let me stay here." Angel wasn't about to open up to her even if it meant her life. "Call Pablo, he will straighten it out."

"If I don't know you, then you're random, and Pablo wouldn't let some random bitch stay here. No pussy in the world is that damn good." The woman said looking at her vibrating phone. "Bueno." She answered as she walked into another room.

Angel felt one of the men staring at her. She completely forgot that she was standing there with nothing but a towel wrapped around her.

"Can I at least have my dignity back and put some clothes on?" She asked with her attitude on a hundred. None of the men responded. Pablo's daughter came back into the living room. She motioned for the guys to put their guns away.

"So, you were locked up with my cousin, huh?" She asked as she took a seat on the couch. That confirmed to Angel that she was speaking Pablo on the phone.

"Look, we can talk, but I need to put on some clothes."

Pablo's daughter laughed when she noticed the towel. "Sorry about that, can't be too careful, you know?"

Angel smirked. *I'm going to have to keep a close eye on this little bitch.* She thought as she headed up the stairs.

When Angel returned to the living room, Pablo's daughter was sitting on the couch watching a movie. Angel took a seat at the opposite end of the sofa.

"This any good?" She asked, picking up the DVD case from the coffee table.

Pablo's daughter nodded her head as she turned down the volume with the remote. "Have you found out anything about Trey?" She asked, getting straight to the point.

Angel was shocked at how open Pablo was with is daughter. He must have told her everything.

"It takes time." Angel replied. "Can't just go around asking questions, you know?"

"Depends on who you're asking." She said. "I can help you. Ever since Trey went missing, I made it my life to find him. If I hadn't—" She stopped mid-sentence.

"If you hadn't what?" Angel asked.

"It's not important. But I know Trey is dead. He has to be. There is no way he would be alive and not contact us all this time."

"You talk like you know something." Angel said as she sat back on the couch.

"I got a job at the club he was last seen at," she started. "There's this guy named Kino. The word is him and his boy Iras knows something about Trey's disappearance. But a lot of shit you hear in a strip club is bullshit. I think they may know, but I just don't know how much they know. I'm hoping if I work there long enough, maybe I'll get lucky."

"So what's the rest of your plan?"

"I don't know, but with your help, we can end this shit and get the answers to this mystery. The only thing is you can't tell my father. He wouldn't be too happy with what I'm doing."

"Why not just tell your father what you know and let him handle it?" Angel asked.

"Look, this shit is too complicated. The less my father knows the better! And besides, if it wasn't for me Trey might still—" she paused. "We… we just can't tell him, okay?"

Angel could sense she wasn't being honest with her. She was hiding something. And the fact that she didn't want her dad to find out made Angel even more suspicious. "Okay, but we do this my way."

Pablo's daughter nodded her head. "Fine. And by the way, I'm Meeka…"

CHAPTER ELEVEN

"Oh shit, yes daddy! Right there! Make my pussy cum!" Trina yelled as Buttah rammed his rock hard dick into her lady purse from behind. He gripped both of her ass cheeks and spread them apart so he could see her juices on his shaft as he pumped, getting more intense with each stroke. Buttah reached up, grabbed the back of her neck and smothered her face into the bed, making her more vulnerable.

The light from Buttah's cell phone on the night stand caught his eye. He reached over to grab it without missing a beat.

"Yo, E!" He answered. "When? Wait, what do you mean tonight?" Buttah stopped his strokes and sat on the bed trying to making since of what he was hearing. "E, we never moved this fast. You don't even know this nigga. How you know he's legit?" Buttah asked as he checked the time on his Movado.

Trina crawled around to position herself in front of him. She wrapped her lips around his chocolate stick and sucked on her own juices.

Buttah bit his bottom lip while he watched his dick disappear into her mouth. He tried his hardest to focus on what Eric was saying, but Trina's head game was tight.

"Yea, I'll be ready." He said before ending the call.

Moments later, Trina bought him to his peak and he let off a well needed nut. Trina made sure it didn't go to waste.

It was almost 9 P.M, and Eric was coming to pick him up at eleven. Their trip to meet a new connect was moved up to tonight. Last month's trip to Miami bought some unwanted company, well at least that's what Buttah thought. They showed some beach property to a man named Gomez. Buttah could tell he was connected, and by the way he spoke, it was obvious he done his homework. He mentioned the name Sweeds and had Eric's attention from that point on. Sweeds was Eric's Brazilian connect. It wasn't easy to get close to Sweeds; in fact he went by an alias of Gator. To know him by Sweeds meant one thing, you worked for him. Gomez offered to charge fifty percent less than what Sweeds charged, for the same quality. Eric didn't want to be disloyal, but he would be a fool to pass that up. Buttah hated the way Eric still made amateur moves. It was like they were young boys all over again. Buttah thought back to the night they were almost killed because of Eric's carelessness.

Summer of 1987

"Fuck!" Eric yelled in frustration. "How the fuck those niggas almost catch us slipping? Buttah, where the hell is ya piece?" Eric looked over at his friend who was lighting a blunt he pulled from behind his ear.

"We need to get to the car. And calm the hell down, you still breathing ain't you?" Buttah replied, exhaling smoke.

Buttah was Eric's right hand man. They were just alike but also like night and day. They were more than friends, they were brothers. Eric and is older brother Isaiah met Buttah when they first moved to southwest Philly. They've been tight ever since, even after the death of Isaiah, Buttah took a special interest of keeping Eric under his wing.

Buttah was a few years older than Eric and even at the age of 22, Buttah had a wise soul. He not only knew the streets, he was the streets.

Without saying a word, Buttah started walking back towards the movie theater. They weren't too far away and at 2:15am walking back to the car was their only option. Eric shook his head not knowing what was going on in his friend's mind as he followed behind. They walked for about fifteen minutes, both keeping their eyes wide open for any pop up visitors. If anybody wanted them dead, right now would be the perfect time to do it because they were both as naked as a newborn baby.

By the time they reached the movie theater, no one was out there. Buttah spotted his black jeep and noticed bullet holes on the passenger side door. Buttah opened the door and looked in the glove compartment for his gun. He pulled out a semiautomatic pistol and cocked it back making sure it was loaded. Eric came up behind him feeling under the seat for his piece. Both guys, feeling a little safer because they were both strapped, hopped into the jeep.

"When did we start jumping in the back of anybody's ride?" Buttah asked, breaking their silence.

"Man, be glad they pulled up." Eric replied. "We could be dead right now."

"If it wasn't for you befriending that nigga Corey, this shit wouldn't have happen. He's a stick-up-kid. They are only loyal to themselves. You of all people should know that."

Eric didn't respond to his friend's comment. He knew that it was his fault, but damn if he was about to admit it.

Buttah chuckled and shook his head. Eric was a hot head. "Man, just remember its bitches out here that's just as grimy as a nigga."

"Ain't no bitch out here got what it takes to step to me that way!" Eric said, smiling. "And besides, it can't be all bad if it looks so good."

"Yea, okay." Buttah uttered, knowing Eric had a lot to learn. "Now, let's dead this nigga Corey." Buttah pulled out of the parking spot. "It's about to be a long night."

"You leaving me, baby?" Trina asked, breaking through Buttah's thoughts.

Buttah looked back at Trina who was now lying on her back and massaging her clit, indicating that she wanted more.

"I'll be back in a couple of days." Buttah said.

"I got to wait a couple days for my dick?"

"Your dick?"

"Yea...It is mines, right?" Trina asked with a stern look on her face as if she knew he was going to agree.

Buttah shook his head at the way she put claim on him. She was young and thought she had Buttah wrapped around her fingers. Her 25-year-old mentality was no match for his 45 years' experience. Buttah had been into young girls since the death of his girlfriend, Mary. She was the only one who captured his heart, and when his 14 year relationship came to an end, Buttah never opened his heart to another woman. He was old-school and knew just how to keep a young bitch in check.

"Alright ma, whatever you say." Buttah said, laughing. He got up and walked over to his dresser. He opened the top drawer and pulled out a rolled up knot of hundred dollar bills and threw it on the bed.

"You'll be good until I get back. But while I'm gone, pick up a few things for my house and get some food in here."

Trina picked up the cash and estimated it was about five grand. She only needed a couple hundred for food shopping. Trina was good at following instructions and planned to do just what he asked.

"Ok, daddy!" She nodded.

Buttah left the room to prepare for in out-of-town trip. Even though he had bad feelings about this, he wasn't about to let Eric go alone. One thing he learned over the years was, *rushed* and *business* never mixed, but good or bad, he was going to be ready.

****

"Mmmmm, is this how you like it, baby?" Meeka asked as she slow grinded on Kino, giving him the best lap dance he'd ever had. Meeka danced topless wearing nothing but a red laced thong and red Gucci pumps. It wasn't the first time she danced for him, but it was the first time she didn't make him pay. It was all part of the plan. She had to get closer if she ever wanted to find out the truth about her cousin, Trey. Meeka straddle him as the song came to an end.

"Times up." She whispered in his ear.

"So, you mean I got to give all this up now?" Kino asked as he massaged her thighs.

"For now…" She smiled.

Kino had yet to have his way with her. Over the past couple of months, every move he made, Meeka shut him down. He was surprised when she finally came on to him. Kino knew it was a matter of time. He stopped his chase with her to pursue another woman that started working in the club. But just like a woman to demand the attention back once it's not on her anymore.

Meeka strapped on her bra and headed to the door, gesturing for Kino to follow.

"So that's it?" Kino asked walking towards her. His dick was hard as a rock and all he could think about was getting inside of her goods.

"It doesn't have to be." Meeka replied. She couldn't stand playing this role. Inside, she wanted to let a round off on his ass just thinking about Trey.

"You rolling with me then?" He asked moving in closer. He had a way of demanding without saying much.

"Let me change first." Meeka said with the look of seduction.

Kino's manhood throbbed for her, and he couldn't wait to get up inside her.

Angel was sitting at the bar sipping on Vodka and lime when she spotted Meeka and Kino coming from the back of the club. She wanted to get a good look at the guy she possibly was going to murder. She took one more sip and tipped the bar tender before heading out. When she got into the car, Angel pulled out her cell phone and sent Meeka a text message.

Ha; this is going to be a breeze! I'm in the car, let's go!

Angel waited for Meeka to appear. Minutes passed and Meeka still had yet to come out of the club. Angel checked her cell phone to see if she texted her back, but there was no message. She dialed Meeka's phone just as she spotted her coming out of the club with Kino. She watched as they both got into a red Acura and pulled off.

What the fuck is this bitch doing? Angel thought. She called Meeka again only to receive her voicemail. Angel started the car and followed behind them. She kept her distance to assure she wouldn't be spotted. Angel had no idea what Meeka was doing, but had every intention to check her about it later. Angel only agreed to work with Meeka with the understanding that she ran the show, and there had to be good communication. Angel had a lot riding on this and was in no hurry to go back to jail over Meeka's carelessness.

Meeka closed her cell phone after sending Angel's call to voicemail for the third time. She knew Angel was going to be pissed because she said she would follow her lead, but this was the first time she would be with Kino outside of the club. She didn't want to pass on the opportunity; Angel would just have to understand.

"I'll get to see how you're living, huh?" Meeka asked. She paid close attention to the route they took, not knowing Angel was following them.

"No not tonight. I got family in town, and it's crowed at my place." Kino lied. He never let anyone from the club know where he rested his head.

"So then where are we going?"

"The Plateau."

"We're going there this late?" Meeka looked over at Kino.

"You scared?"

"Hell yea, we are in Kill-adelphia!"

"If you're with me, you're good. I'm kind of a big deal in these streets." Kino stated.

"Funny, I've never heard of you." Meeka said, jokingly.

"Oh really, you never heard of the cat killer?" He asked.

"The cat killer? Why the hell do they call you that?"

"Because I murder the pussy!"

Meeka burst into laughter at how corny Kino sounded. "What? Kino you are so whack!"

"Damn you laughing at me, ma?" Kino said, laughing as well. He looked over at Meeka. That was the first time he actually noticed how beautiful she was. When she smiled, it exposed her dimples, which added an innocent touch to her.

"You got to do me one favor." Kino said.

"What's that?"

"Next time you dance for me, I want to hear you speak that Spanish shit."

Meeka chuckled. "My Spanish isn't even all that good. I can understand it better. I'm Rican and black."

When they pulled up to the plateau, it was like a ghost town.

The dimly lit park was a beautiful tourist spot during the day. But at night, if you were out there it was a good chance you could be robbed, rapped, or even killed. The best place to view the city was there. You could see downtown and all the high-rise buildings. The lights from the buildings lit up the night's sky. It was a shame that such a beautiful place was also the craziest. The parked was closed off after certain hours but they parked there anyway.

"You blow?" Meeka asked pulling out a sandwich bag that held little nickel packs of weed. She had to find a way to get his mind off of sex and into a conversation.

"That ain't all I do." He said looking down at her perfectly toned legs.

"Well roll up then," Meeka smiled. She threw the bag on his lap.

Kino wasn't expecting to chill, but he never turned down free weed. He reached over, opened his glove compartment and pulled out two blunt wraps. Meeka turned on the light so she could check herself in the mirror.

Kino glanced over at Meeka. Outside of the club she looked like a normal girl, in fact, he couldn't see why such a beautiful girl had to do such a degrading job. She was prettier than most girls he dealt with.

"You good?" Meeka said when she peeped how Kino stopped rolling up and stared at her.

"I'm always good, ma."

Meeka shook her head and turned off the light.

"So what's your deal?" He asked, licking the blunt to seal it shut.

"What you mean?"

"What makes a girl like you want to strip?"

Meeka laughed. "A girl like me? And what's that supposed to mean?"

"You seem like the type of girl that should be up in some college doing something with your life."

"What makes you think I'm not?"

"Are you?"

"No, but I could be if I wanted to." Meeka lied.

"My point exactly," Kino nodded. "So why do you choose to strip?"

Got'em! Meeka thought. The conversation was going just the way she planned. "It's a long story."

"We've got time." Kino said lighting his homemade cigarette.

"Sometimes we do things because we have to and not because we want to." Meeka started. "My mom has a problem. One that almost ended her life. When my dad passed away he left a savings for us. I told my mom about the stash he kept in the house because she was going to need it. At the time, I had no idea she was a gambler. Not even a day after I told her, she took all of it and went to some underground spot called the Dungeon."

"Your mom was at Smoke's place?" Kino asked. "That place is bad news. If you don't know how Smoke gets down, it's better to say far away."

"Who you telling? I came home one day and that nigga had my mom tied up and lying face down. I just knew she was dead. Before I could ask what was going on, some guy grabbed me. He kept asking where the money was. I was scared to tell them because I knew soon as they got what they wanted, they would have killed our asses. At that time, I had no idea she used all of it. I begged him not to hurt us and promised I would get whatever it is he was looking for. I made a deal to get back whatever she owed him."

"Word?" Kino was shocked.

Meeka slowly nodded. "I guess he thought I was the only way he would ever see any of the money she owed him, so he told me if I ever wanted to see her breathing again I would have forty thousand to him in a month. That's when I started working at the club. I knew I could make some quick money. When the month was up, all I made was about five thousand. I gave him what I had and he said he would keep her alive as long as I kept paying." Meeka had no idea where that story came from, but she made it sound good.

After hearing her background, Kino was turned off to wanting to sleep with her. He felt an urge to want to protect her. It was like she was an innocent little girl not knowing what she'd gotten herself into. Kino didn't know how to respond. He knew he should just mind his own business, but after talking to her, he couldn't help the feeling of wanting to help her.

"Just so you know, anytime you want to quit the club you can." He said looking straight ahead at the city lights.

Meeka looked over at him and could tell that he was serious. "Quit? I can't. I got to do what I got to do. My mother's life is a stake."

Kino knew Smoke. He knew the chances of her mother being alive were very low, but he wasn't about to put that thought in her head. "We can figure out a way to get your mom back, but for now, I don't want you working at the club."

"Why do you even care?" Meeka asked.

Kino didn't know how to answer her. He didn't even know why. He just felt the need to. "Just know that from now on, I got you. You don't have shit to worry about."

Damn! No, no, no! Stay focused, Meeka. Trey is your blood. Fuck this nigga. She thought to herself. She knew he meant every word he said. It's rare to come across a guy like him. The thought of her falling for Kino would only complicate things.

"If you were around a real nigga in the first place, you wouldn't be in this mess." Kino added as he took another drag.

Meeka saw another side of Kino. She wasn't sure what her next move would be, but she had to get it done and over with. The more she spent time with him, it would make it harder for her to end his life if it came down to it.

Maybe I should have just fucked him. At least then, we wouldn't be in here getting all deep. Meeka thought as she sat back in the seat and mellowed out the rest of the night.

CHAPTER TWELVE

"I knew it! A fucking bitch!" Loyal yelled in frustration. "How is he going to play me like that? I had his back since day one."

Melissa listened as she heard her friend breaking down over the phone. She knew it was going to hurt her to tell her what she was seeing at that very moment.

"They stopped in front of the boutique." Melissa said, not taking her eyes off of Iras and his lady companion. "Let me call you right back."

"What? No! Melissa, don't say anything to him. I need to figure out my—"

"I'm not saying shit to them, but I am going in to see what's up. Consider this insurance." Melissa said before closing her cell phone. She hid behind a pair of dark shades and a large, black, floppy sunhat. She made sure they were in the store before getting out of her car. Being spotted by Iras would throw salt on her plans right now. She'd been following him for two days and this was the first time she saw him with another woman. She needed to get closers to find out what was going on.

Melissa got out her car and walked across the street to the boutique. She spotted them immediately when she entered and headed in their direction, keeping her face lowered. She made her way to a rack nearby and began looking through it with her back towards them. From where she was positioned, she could hear their entire conversation.

"Are you sure this is a good idea?" Monica asked Iras as she looked through the rack of dresses. "I don't think it's the right time for your father and me to meet yet." She came across a blue dress and she held it up against her, admiring the fabric.

"My dad needs to know. He'll just have to understand this is my life and he ain't running you out like I let him do with a lot of other shit."

"What about Loyal? Will she be there?"

"Yea, she will. I'm not sure how she's going to react but she's a big girl. She'll get over it."

Mutha fucka! Melissa thought. *He is taking her to meet his father!*

The news shot threw Melissa's body like lighting. She instantly felt the urge to beat the shit out of the both of them.

"May I help you?" The store associate asked Melissa.

"Oh no, that's ok. I'm just looking."

"Well, we have a great sale going on today." Melissa couldn't hear the rest of their conversation; she tried to get rid of the store associate who was unknowingly interrupting her ease dropping.

"If I need anything, I will ask!" Melissa blurted out.

The woman backed off after sensing Melissa's attitude. When Melissa looked over her shoulder, Iras was gone. She wasn't sure where he went because of the annoying store worker. The woman he was with was still there. She had three dresses on her arm as she headed towards the fitting room. Melissa followed her. She wanted to scare the shit out her, and had to make it quick because Iras could pop up any second.

This bitch thinks she can play my friend, she got another thing coming. Melissa thought.

The woman stopped in her tracks when she passed a rack with designer scarves. Melissa pulled a random shirt from the closest rack to her so she wouldn't look obvious.

"Excuse me!" Monica called for the store associate.

Melissa stood a couple feet away. She got a good look at the woman and froze. Her heart began to race and her breathing rapidly sped up. She wanted to run out, but her body and mind was having a disagreement. Anger filled her body as her eyes filled with tears. Melissa dropped the shirt and turned to run out of the store, bumping into racks and causing the attention to be on her. She jumped into her car and pulled off as if she just broken out of jail.

*****

It had been two days since Angel followed Meeka and Kino to the park, where she drifted off to sleep. She was woken up by a homeless man the next morning when he tapped on her window, asking for change. She hadn't seen or heard from her since, and Meeka had yet to answer any of her text messages.

Angel laid across her bed collecting her thoughts when she heard the front door slam.

"Bout time!" Angel said as she jumped up and headed down stairs. "Where the hell have you—" Angel stopped mid-sentence when she saw Pablo standing there and not Meeka.

"You are expecting someone else?" Pablo said with his strong Spanish accent.

"As a matter of fact I was. Meeka didn't come here last night and I got a little worried." Angel said.

"One thing you'll learn about my daughter is that she will make it hard to keep tabs on her, even for her father. She checks in with me every day, she went back to school, so you probably won't be seeing her for a while."

Angel knew Meeka didn't go back to school. What she told her father was a flat out cover up, but Angel went along with the story.

"So how are you making out?" Pablo asked her as he sat down on the couch.

Angel stood at the staircase, trying to feel him out. It was the first time he engaged in a conversation with her. He was out of town so much she almost forgot what he looked like.

"I'm managing," she responded. "Not too much news yet, though."

Pablo had no clue his daughter was in on helping her find Trey's killer, and she wasn't going to be the one to tell him.

"Don't stress yourself too much; my sister is already coming to the realization of her son. I told her so many times to move back home to Miami. Her being out here wasn't any good for the kids." Pablo said, thinking about Teresa and Trey.

"Is that why you're here?"

"When my sister wanted to leave Miami, I knew where ever she went it wasn't going to be an easy move. She had just buried her husband, and I guess being out there wasn't for her anymore." Pablo said, lighting a cigar. "Do you mind?"

Angel shook her head, no.

"I bought this house when she moved out here. I came often to visit until she was comfortable enough to be on the East coast alone."

"Where is she now?"

"Back home."

"Miami?"

"Puerto Rico," Pablo answered. "Since Trey went missing, I didn't want her out here until I found out who's behind this."

Angel thought about Meeka. For someone who seemed so tight about his family, his daughter was running the streets and he didn't even know.

"I really do appreciate you letting me stay here, and I'm trying my best to find out what I can." Angel said.

"I don't bite. You can come have a seat on the couch if you like." He said gesturing for her to sit down.

"I was going to make something to eat first. Are you hungry?" Angel asked.

"I'm always hungry."

"You want tacos?"

"Why, because I'm Puerto Rican?" Pablo said laughing.

Angel had to laugh too when she realized that was the exact reason she asked him.

"I'm sorry, I didn't mean to offend you." She said. "How about Alfredo?"

"Alfredo would be nice." Pablo nodded.

Angel whipped up a delicious chicken Alfredo with buttered dinner rolls and a glass of Mascato completed the meal. Pablo kept Angel laughing most of the night. They had a lot more in common than she thought. She found out Meeka's mother is black and she wanted nothing to do with Meeka when she caught Pablo cheating on her.

"I can't see myself giving up my baby. Not over something stupid like that." Angel said. "If anything, I'm leaving and taking her with me."

"It's too many little girls and not enough women." Pablo said. "Meeka was well taken care off. She's better off with me. That is the only woman I would die for."

"The only person I've ever felt like that over was my grandmother; she was my *everything*."

"God only offers you a few people like that in a lifetime; that unconditional love." Pablo said, sipping his drink.

"Well, hopefully he spares me one more chance." Angel said. She was feeling a bit buzzed from drinking. She didn't know if it was the alcohol making her feel comfortable or if it was his charm. She never felt like that around a man. Anytime she was around a man, either she was getting paid for her goods or getting robbed of them.

Pablo was feeling it as well. He didn't plan on being there that long, but time got away from him. He was enjoying her company.

"I could go for a good movie right now." Pablo said.

"Yea that sounds good," Angel agreed. "I'll clean up while you find something."

"No leave it, cleaning can wait until the morning." Pablo said as he got up and grabbed both of their drinks.

Angel hesitated when she saw Pablo heading towards the steps. "Aren't we going to watch a movie?"

"Movies are always better in my room. The best equipment will make you feel like you're in the movie."

Angel's defense mode started to kick in. She discreetly looked around for something she could protect herself with.

"Is something wrong?" Pablo asked from the top of the stairs.

Angel relax, you're a big girl now. She thought to herself. "No. nothing's wrong." she responded, coming up the steps behind him.

Pablo unlocked his bedroom door. That room was the only room in the house Angel hadn't seen. It'd been locked since she moved in. Her eyes widened with shock when she walked it. Not that she was impressed by the fancy layout, but because she wasn't expecting it to be decked out the way he had it. It was indeed the ultimate bachelor's pad. A king sized bed, a leather love seat, mini bar, recessed lighting, and a fifty inch flat screen were just a few of the luxuries the room held.

When Pablo turned on the television, the movie Scarface instantly came on. He sat on the bed and took off his shoes. Angel shut the door and sat on the other side of the bed. Pablo pressed a button on the remote and speakers rose up on the head board. He pressed another button and the lights went out, making it a more comfortable environment. He sat back on the bed leaning his back against the headboard and picked up his drink.

Angel was on her P's and Q's, just in case he stepped out of line. She sat back on the bed as well and focused on the featured film.

"So tell me something, how did a beautiful woman like you get into a situation that sent her to prison?"

Angel never expected Pablo to ask about her sentence. "I've wondered about that a lot over the years." She replied.

"And what's the answer?"

Angel shrugged. "I'm not sure there is one. But I do know I've learned a lot in jail. Most people would think I missed all of life's lessons, but the same shit that went on in there, I'm pretty sure went on out here. I know who I am, what I want, and what I won't go for. That's all that matters."

"That's a good way of looking at," Pablo said, nodding his head.

They spent the rest of the night talking until they both drifted off to sleep. It was almost four a.m. and Angel laid curled up in Pablo's arms.

She woke up from the sound of a passing car honking its horn. She was a light sleeper, especially when she was in prison. Angel looked up at a sleeping Pablo. The room was dark and the only light was coming from the street lights peering through the sheer curtains. Angel didn't remember falling asleep. She woke up expecting to be naked and stretched out, but to her surprise, she wasn't. She was getting the sense that Pablo was a pure gentleman. He hadn't even come on to her. It felt good to be around a man with more intentions then just getting some ass. Hell, it felt good to be around anyone other than the inmates. Angel turned on her other side.

"Are you ok?" Pablo asked.

Angel had no idea he was awake. "Yes. I'm sorry, did I wake you?"

"No, I don't sleep much at night." Pablo said.

"It's the best time for me to clear my mind. I do a little praying, too."

"Maybe I could use some of that." Angel said, sarcastically. "You'd be surprised at what a little prayer will do. He may even spare you another chance at love."

"Yeah, maybe…" Angel said. She brushed off the prayer thing. "My grandmother used to always tell me prayer is simply talking to God. You tell him your problems, and he will make them better. Well he must not care too much about me, because my problems damn sure haven't gone away."

"Just because you ask him to take them away, doesn't mean that he will." Pablo replied. "Life is a classroom, and our problems are lessons. When you learn it, then it goes away. God give us opportunity to make the right choices. And most of the time we don't, so our problems reoccur."

How could a man who does so much dirty work, be so deep into god? Angel thought. It didn't make sense to her, but it didn't matter. She felt good being around Pablo, and his good looks was a plus. He wasn't the average eye candy. He had an older, more mature look. His skin was clear and smooth, and he had the best teeth Angel had ever seen. Angel wasn't looking to get serious with anyone any time soon, but Pablo was defiantly the type of man she needed in her life.

"Will you pray with me?" Angel asked.

Without saying a word, Pablo reached for her hands and closed them inside of his. They prayed together as Angel was slowly started falling for him.

CHAPTER THIRTEEN

"Damn girl, you in there making the clothes?" Kino asked Meeka, waiting for her to come out of the dressing room.

"Be quiet. I'm almost done." Meeka replied. "I look good too!"

"I'll be the judge of that." Kino said, jokingly.

Meeka walked out of the dressing room wearing a black Michael Kors two piece bathing suit and a black sheer cover-up.

Damn! Kino thought.

"How does it look, too much?" Meeka asked.

"I like it. Just like the others you've tried on."

"Just *like*? Kino I need to look good on the beach, ok. So while I'm hanging off your arm, the other niggas will be wishing they were you."

Kino smiled. He knew Meeka was a handful, but he was feeling her. Ever since the night in the car three weeks ago, they spent most of their time together. Kino even decided to take her on a small vacation to get away from all of her drama. They were leaving for the Bahamas in the morning and they were out shopping, picking up some last minute items.

"Look ma, you look good in anything you wear. Just get whatever you need so we can go. I got something important to handle tonight." Kino told her looking at his watch.

"I guess I'm just going to have to take them all." Meeka said walking back into the dressing room. *What the hell am I doing?* She thought.

Meeka was caught up. She didn't want it to happen, but Kino snuck his way in her heart. He was the total opposite of who she thought he was. She'd been with him damn near every day and still hasn't gotten any information on Trey. Hopefully, this trip would open him up. She just hoped she would be able to pull through with her plans if Kino really was behind Trey's murder. Things would have been so much easier if she would have kept in contact with Angel. She hadn't spoken to her since the night at the club, nearly a month ago.

I'll call her tonight to catch her up. She thought. Meeka finished up in the dressing room and headed out.

****

Loyal laid across the bed consumed in her thoughts. It had been weeks since she spoke with her friend Melissa. Every time she tried to call, it would go straight to voicemail. She even stopped passed her house a few times but still wasn't able to get her. Loyal felt hurt. Melissa was her best friend, and the only person who she could really talk to. Now all of a sudden she disappeared. Something wasn't right, and Loyal could feel it in her gut.

The last time they spoke, Melissa saw Iras with another woman. Loyal's emotions were all over the place. She couldn't stand to be around Iras, but at the same time didn't want him out of her sight. She never mentioned his infidelity to him, and how could she with no solid proof. She tried her hardest to keep things normal between them, but whenever he was near her she would get an instant attitude. Tonight was the night of a family dinner they'd planned a while back.

Loyal was in no mood for company, but was hoping this was something she needed to take her mind of off things. Iras had gone out food shopping for this event and she stayed back to clean up. Everything was ready for tonight.... except Loyal. She planned to get through the night with a bottle Vodka.

****

Kino sat in his car outside of the Dungeon. It's been a while since he had a run in with Smoke, and he couldn't believe what he was about to do. Normally, he wouldn't be caught dead there after what went down, but this was something he had to do. The sun had begun to set. Kino waited over an hour before he saw Smoke's car pull up. He watched Smoke get out of the car with three other men and headed into his facility. Kino grabbed his bag from the floor and tucked his gun under his seat before getting out. He knew they would check him for a gun if he wanted to talk to Smoke. Kino walked into the Dungeon and was stopped at the door.

"Bag check!" The door man said.

"I'm here to see Smoke."

The guy took his bag, and another guy came from behind patting him down.

"Tell him it's Kino."

The doorman didn't respond. He walked through the curtains that led to Smoke's office. Moments later, he reappeared.

"Follow me." He said. Kino picked up his backpack and did just that. The doorman walked half way and stopped. He pointed to Smoke's office door gesturing for Kino to go in.

The doorman pulled out two hand guns and cocked them back. The sound of the guns caught Kino's attention and he turned back to look at him. That was his way of letting Smoke's man know he wasn't impressed. Kino knocked on the door.

"You may enter." A voice said.

Kino opened the door and saw Smoke sitting at his desk receiving a massage by a topless beauty.

"Mr. Kino! To what do I owe this surprise?"

Kino didn't say anything. He looked at the woman and then back at Smoke.

"Oh, this must be serious." Smoke said, flagging his hand in the air.

The woman stopped what she was doing and walked out the room.

"So, what can I do for you?"

Kino threw the backpack on the desk. "I'm here to tell you, Meeka doesn't work for you anymore. This should cover your losses."

Smoke opened the backpack and smiled at the stacks of money.

"She doesn't owe you shit now, so lay off." Kino finished.

Smoke got up and walked around to the front of the desk. He picked up a cigar from his case and lit it. "Well, I'm flattered youngin'. But as generous as this is, I can't take it. I don't know what you're talking about."

"Come on Smoke, cut the bullshit—"

"Aye, aye," Smoke cut him off. "Watch your tone in my office. Now I told you I don't what you're talking about."

"I'm talking about Meeka, the girl you got working for you to pay her mother's gambling debt. Knowing you, her mother's dead by now, but—"

"Now hold on there, youngin. I don't need any extra bodies added to my count. And that's not my style, working off a debt, this ain't a bank. Where in hell are you getting this information from…"

****

The house smelled good from all the food and the kitchen counter top over flowed from all of the bottles of liquor lined up. Loyal already had three cups and didn't plan on stopping anytime soon.

"Smells good. I'm hungry, already." Iras said walking into the kitchen.

Loyal stood at the sink with her back towards him.

Iras came behind her and slid his arms around her waistline. "I got a surprise for you." Iras said, kissing her on the neck. Loyal didn't respond. All she could think about was Iras holding another bitch the same way he held her.

"I need to freshen up." Loyal said, breaking away from his hold. "People will be here soon." She walked to the bathroom and shut the door. She stared at herself in the mirror. Loyal was beat. No matter how much make up she applied, she still looked mentally and emotionally exhausted. Her worries had begun to take a toll on her. She pulled out her cell phone and dialed Melissa's number. She wasn't expecting her to show up tonight, but she was hoping that she would at least answer her phone.

"Hey you've reached Melissa, leave a message after the...."

Loyal hung up the phone. *With or without proof, I need to confront his ass.* She thought. She opened the door to the bathroom just as she heard the doorbell ring.

****

Angel sat at the table with Pablo and his aquatints. The group enjoyed dinner at Castello's as Pablo talked business with his new partners. Angel felt her phone vibrating through her clutch. She opened it and looked at the caller ID.

"Excuse me, I need to take this." She told the group as she got up from the table. Quickly, she walked to the ladies restroom and answered the phone. "Where the fuck have you been?"

"Damn, hello to you too!" Meeka said, sarcastically.

"Meeka, do you know how worried I've been? You don't answer my calls, you haven't been home... Where are you?" Angel asked in a demanding tone, while trying to keep her voice low.

"I'm at Kino's house. I've been staying with him." Meeka admitted.

Angel's blood boiled. She wanted to snatch her hard headed ass threw the phone.   "Where does he live, we need to talk face-to-face?"

"Just meet me at the park on Wynnefield Avenue near the college. I'll be there at six." Meeka said before hanging up.

Angel looked at her phone and shook her head. Meeka had some nerve. It was already 5:15pm. Angel didn't want to miss meeting her, so she had to go.

When she emerged from the restroom, Angel saw the men all standing up. She approached the table just as they we saying their goodbyes.

"Is everything ok?" Pablo asked.

"Yes, everything is fine. Are we done here?" Angel asked.

Pablo nodded. "Yes, we are."

"It was so nice meeting you, Eric." Angel said as she extended her hand.

"The pleasure was all mines," Eric responded. "And Mr. Gomez...."

"Please, call me Pablo." Pablo insisted.

"Pablo, Buttah will be in touch with you in a few days."

Pablo looked at Buttah. "You don't say much, I see."

Eric looked at Buttah knowing he had his reservations about Pablo.

"I'll be in touch in a few days." Buttah confirmed.

"All is well then." Pablo said.

They all walked out of the restaurant and parted their separate ways.

Eric and Buttah got into Eric's car.

"You going over to Ras' tonight?" Eric asked.

"I don't trust this Pablo nigga, and he brings his bitch along?" Buttah said ignoring Eric's question.

Eric pulled off without saying anything.

"I hope you know what you're doing." Buttah said before putting on his shades and turning up the music.

****

Angel and Pablo pulled up to a hotel in downtown Philadelphia. He had a few more things to handle in the city before heading back over the New Jersey Bridge.

"Pablo," Angel said. "I have to make run and I need to use the car."

"Um, Ok…" He replied, completely caught off guard. "What time will you be back? I have planned a night for us."

"I won't be long. I promise."

Pablo got out of the car and waited until she got in the driver's seat to shut her door. As much as he wanted to ask her where she had to go all of a sudden, he didn't. It wasn't his place to ask, and Angel was free to go and come as she pleased. She backed up out the driveway and headed straight to the park to meet Meeka.

When she arrived, she spotted Meeka walking up the sidewalk wearing a white jogging suit with the hood pulled up and a pair of dark sun glasses.

Angel pulled to the side of her and rolled down the window. Without saying a word Meeka got into the car.

"Before you get mad, let me explain." Meeka pleaded.

"Meeka cut the bullshit!" Angel yelled. "You expect me to just be okay with the stunt you pulled? You running around here playing girlfriend, I bet you aren't even close to finding out about Trey. You do still remember him right?"

"Don't come at me like that!" Meeka snapped back. "Trey is my blood. MY BLOOD! You're the outsider. Remember that!"

It took everything in Angel not to smack the taste out of Meeka's mouth. She bit her bottom lip and gained her composure. Angel looked over at Meeka. She had a glow to her that Angel had never seen before. As if she was in a happy place. She looked at her attire. Meeka was laced and since she knew Pablo has not spoken to her, she must have gotten it from Kino. Angel laughed to herself.

"What the hell is so funny?" Meeka asked.

"You're fucking that nigga!"

"What? No I'm not!"

Angel could see right through her. "This is over. I will handle it from here."

"Over?" Meeka said. "Who are you to tell me when something's over. I'm close, I can feel it, and after this Bahamas vacation I will know all I need to know."

"Bahamas? So you are going away with this nigga now? You cannot be this stupid, Meeka. I guess this is what I get for having a little girl do a woman's job."

"If it wasn't for this little girl, you would have no leads in the first place. I'm the one taking the biggest risk!"

"No one told you to move in with him, Meeka. You fucked up our whole plan. And don't think you're going out of the country with him. I will tell your father."

"I'm grown, Angel. I can handle myself." Meeka said before getting out the car and slamming the door. She began to walk back to Kino's house. She didn't want to admit it, but Angel was right. Her feelings for Kino had gotten real... too real.

"Oh, I know her alright. But she doesn't work for me." Smoke said as they watched Meeka getting out of a car. Kino brought Smoke to his house to meet Meeka, but when they saw her come out of the house looking nervous and suspicious, they followed her to a park minutes away from Kino's house.

Red flags went up in Kino's head. One thing he knew about Smoke was that he didn't lie about his money, but he didn't want to believe Meeka lied to him about her past.

"How do you know her Smoke?" Kino asked.

"I did a little business with her father, once upon a time." Smoke started. "And let me tell you, they don't call themselves Death Trap Mafia for nothing. They are only loyal to their kind. I don't get down like that. So we made a mutual agreement to part ways respectfully."

Hearing the name *Death Trap Mafia* instantly turned on Kino's pit bull instinct. He was all too familiar with them. Especially the one they rocked to sleep…Trey.

"Youngin', whatever business you got with this bitch, you better dig a little deeper. Word on the street is one of their own is missing. I don't know what's going on, but that story she fed you was a bunch of garbage."

Kino pulled off without saying a word. Rage filled his body. Meeka was setting him up. She had to be. But what made it worst was that he hadn't caught on to her sooner.

How the fuck did I let this shit slip passed me? He thought. After dropping Smoke off, he headed straight to Iras' house.

"Her ass want to play the game like a nigga, she can get rocked like one, too…"

CHAPTER FOURTEEN

The music was flowing and the mood was chilled. Close friends and family started to arrive at Iras and Loyal's place. Loyal was buzzed. She had been drinking all night; especially after meeting Iras' surprise guest of the evening, Monica. She had no idea that Iras was contacting her. She put her feelings on pause, because she didn't want to make a scene in front of Monica, or anyone else.

She watched Monica and Iras as the two stepped in the living room. They seemed to be close. Even though this was all new to her, Loyal was going to try and build a relationship with Monica as well. She never saw Iras smile so much, especially in the last month. It was as if Monica was the missing piece in his life.

The doorbell rang and Loyal went to answer it.

"Hey, you made it." Loyal said, hugging Kino.

Monica peered over at the door. "Who's that?" She asked her son.

Iras turned around to see who she was talking about. "My brother from another mother." He responded.

"Does your brother have to hug your woman like that?" Monica asked.

"Ha." Iras brushed off her comment. "Come on, I'll introduce you."

"My nigga!" Iras said as he walked up on his best friend.

"Yo bro!" Kino responded.

"I'd like you to meet someone." Iras smiled. "This is Monica."

"Mom dukes?" Kino said. "Nice to finally meet you. I've heard a lot about you.

"That makes one of us…" Loyal said in a low tone.

Monica pretended she didn't hear Loyal's comment.

"Put that hand away and give me a hug. Any friend of my boy is a friend of mines. Are you hungry? We got tons of food." Monica said walking Kino to the kitchen.

"*We* got tons of food?" Loyal said to Iras.

"Don't start, babe. She means well."

Loyal shook her head and walked away to engage in the rest of their guest.

About an hour passed and everyone was having a good time; everyone except Kino. Meeka was on his mind, heavy. He thought back to the day he saw her getting into the car with the with the DT marks on it.

Why didn't I realize that shit then? What was I thinking?

He thought of them sending Meeka as a set up, but it wouldn't have taken this long for the ball to drop.

What if it's not a set up? What if she doesn't know about our beef with her family? If she found out I helped kill Trey, it will crush her. Then, why would she lie to me? Kino battled with his thoughts. If this was any other bitch, there wouldn't have been a question as to what his next move was. But because his feelings ran deep for Meeka, he had to hear it from her mouth.

Iras pulled Loyal to the middle of the floor where a few people were dancing.

"Ras, what are you doing?" Loyal asked. They both had a few drinks and was feeling it, but Loyal was in no mode for dancing.

"You seem a little tense. I'm just trying to help you loosen up." Iras said, dancing to the music.

As Loyal gave into his demand, the song changed to Will Smith's *Summer Time*.

"Whoa, this is my shit!" Monica said dancing over to her son and Loyal. "This song never gets old. You've got to give me this one baby boy."

Monica pulled him away from Loyal. Iras went with the flow, and him and his mother jammed to the song as if it were *their* song. Annoyed, Loyal walked over to where Kino was sitting and sat next to him.

"I need a drink—now!" she said. Without hesitation, she picked up Kino's cup and drunk whatever was in it.

"Take it easy, L." Kino said. He never saw her drink so much in one night. For as long as he'd known her, she was one who drinks the least whenever they were out.

"Kino, this bitch doesn't like me. And she making it obvious. All night she has been going out of her way to get in mines. If she wasn't his mother, I would have been put her ass in her place. And your boy is too dumb to see that shit."

"Just give it time," Kino said trying to make Loyal feel better. "She'll come around."

Loyal put her hand on his shoulder. "Well, until then, I'll cuddle myself with my E&J."

"He's just your boy, huh?" Monica asked as she nodded over to Loyal and Kino sitting on the couch. "Looks a little too close to me."

Iras looked over at the two sitting on the sofa, laughing.

"And what the hell is that funny?" Monica added. "There's only one thing that can make a woman laugh that hard at a man's jokes."

Iras stopped dancing to observe his woman and his best friend.

"I've got to use the little girl's room. I'll be right back." Monica said.

Her words cut him deep. She had him thinking the worst, and the fact that he consumed so much alcohol didn't help.

"You've been quiet all night. What's going on in your head?" Loyal asked Kino.

"I'm just tired. I need to get some air. I'll be back." He said as he got up from the sofa and left out.

Loyal pulled her cell phone out of her jean pocket to check the time. She saw that she had six missed calls. The music was so loud, she didn't even hear her cell phone ringing. She got excited when she saw that it was Melissa. Her phone started ringing again. She flipped it open to answer it.

"Melissa? Hello? Hold on, I can't hear you." Loyal said. She got up to walk out of the condo so she could talk to her friend.

"I can hear you now." Loyal said into the phone. "Where have you been?"

"Loyal, I'm so sorry about leaving. But I really have to tell you something."

"What's wrong? Are you hurt?" Loyal asked as she grew concerned. Melissa didn't sound like her normal self.

Melissa sighed. "I need to see you. I can't talk right now, but I will be back in Philly later on tonight."

"Melissa, where are you?"

"I'll explain later, I promise. Just come by later on tonight." Melissa said before hanging up.

Loyal saw Kino sitting in his car staring straight ahead. She walked up to the car and knocked on the window. Kino unlocked to door and she got in the passenger side.

Iras saw when Loyal stepped out on her cell phone. He watched her threw the window as she got into Kino's car. Iras' anger went from zero to sixty. He went into the bedroom to retrieve his gun.

"I think I need to have a talk with my so called best friend."

"Okay now, what's up? You're quiet all night, you haven't even had one drink, and I know you never pass up alcohol." Loyal said to Kino.

Kino didn't respond.

"It's a woman, ain't it?"

"Since when have you know me to be pressed about a broad?"

Just then, Iras stormed out of the building and down to the car. Neither one of them saw him and was both startled when he banged on the car window.

Kino got out of the car. "What the hell is your problem? You almost broke my fucking glass."

"You're my fucking problem!" Iras hissed, violently pushing Kino in his chest.

Loyal got out of the car and ran around the other side. "Ras, what are doing?"

Iras ignored her. "You fucking my bitch?" He pointed the gun at Kino.

"What!" Loyal said, shocked at his words. "Ain't nobody fucking around!"

"Ras, you're trippin'!" Kino said, backing up.

He didn't want to fight his best friend but was ready if it was going to go down. The whole party seemed to move outside. Two of their mutual friends ran down and grabbed Iras. He tried to pull away, and in the midst, the gun dropped out of his hand.

"Oh, so you're going to shoot me now? That's how it is Ras?" Kino asked.

"Kino, he's just drunk! He'll—"

"Bitch, go ahead defend your man." Iras said to Loyal cutting her off. "I see ya type now."

"My type?" Loyal couldn't believe how he was acting. Iras was always a hot-head, but never with her.

Kino hopped in his car and drove off.

Tears started to form in Loyal's eyes as she turned around to go back in. Monica stood at the steps with a smirk on her face. She straightened up when she saw Loyal watching her. Loyal went inside, grabbed her purse and car keys. She came back out and got in her car and drove off.

Eric arrived at Iras' place and saw a bunch of people standing outside. *What is going on here?* He thought. He got out of the car looking for his son and found more than what he was looking for.

He spotted Monica sitting on the steps with Iras. Monica and Eric locked eyes for the first time in over twenty year. It was a deadly, unspoken, venomous encounter. His soft welcoming eyes turned into hell's fire pit the second he saw her. It was as if a sleeping beast had just awaken. Monica returned the glare, delivering the exact message. To the both of them, it was as if the world had stopped and only the two of them existed, ready to fight the final battle. You couldn't break their stare with the Jaws of Life.

CHAPTER FIFTEEN

Kino dialed Meeka's number as he raced home full speed. First the woman he loved was affiliated with his rivals, now his best friend was accusing him of sleeping with his lady. His emotions where on edge and he needed balance in his life. He needed to hear the truth and he was hoping that Meeka would do just that.

"Hello?" Meeka answered.

"Get dressed. I'm coming to get you."

"Where are we—"

Kino ended the call before she could finish her sentence. He prayed that Smoke was lying, but he was soon about to find out.

****

Eric paced back and forth with both his hands on his hip in Iras' bedroom. Iras sat on the bed smoking his weed.

"So what you thought I was just going to show up here and have a happy reunion?" Eric asked. "How long has she been here?"

Iras could see the veins popping out of his father's neck. He was pissed.

"I'm out. I'm not going to sit here for this bull shit." Iras said getting up from the bed.

Eric pushed him back down. "You're going to sit here, and you will listen!" He demanded. "And because you're intoxicated, I'm going ignore that fact that you think you're man enough to curse at me."

"I seem to be the only man in here."

"What did you say?" Eric said as he took off his suit jacket. He moved in closer to his son waiting for him to respond.

Iras stood back up and met his father face-to-face.

"I'm not the only one who's been keeping secrets." He started. "All this time you're telling me my mother is dead, and now she shows up at my front door."

Eric put his hands on his head and walked over to the window.

"Nothing to say now, huh?" Iras spat.

"I did it to protect you. It's a lot of shit that you don't know about her. I did what a man had to do in order to protect his child."

"How? By taking me from my mother and threatening her life if she ever tried to come for me?"

"Is that what she told you?" Eric said as the anger grew on his face.

"My mother told me all I needed to know— something you never did."

"That bitch is not your mother!" Eric said storming back over to his son. "She was druggie hoe, more concerned about getting a hit instead of her own kid. I was not going to stand by and watch her mess your life up."

The tension in the room was so thick you could cut it with a knife. Monica stood outside the bedroom door taking in everything Eric was saying.

He's right! You were not a good mother to him. He did what was best. No he didn't! He was only thinking about himself, and he took my baby. But Monica, Iras probably wouldn't be alive if he hadn't. Fuck that, he is going to pay for what he did.

Monica ran into the bathroom and splashed some cold water on her face.

"It was the past, you're here now. You have him back." She said out loud as she looked at herself in the mirror. Her words were convincing because the voices in her head faded. She heard a door slam. She opened the bathroom door to see where Iras was. Eric was standing in the middle of the living room floor. He didn't know Monica was still in the condo. He picked up his phone and called Buttah to tell him what just happened. The conversation was short. When Eric hung up the phone and turned to go back into the bedroom to retrieve his jacket, he saw Monica standing there.

"You better not hurt my son." He said, pushing passed her and picking up his jacket off the bed.

"He's my son, too, Eric!"

Eric snapped. He gripped her neck and pinned her to the wall. "You think you can call yourself a mother selling your son for a hit?" Tears formed in Eric's eyes. "Or leaving him at a stranger's house for days and getting so high that you couldn't remember where you left him."

Monica tried to release his grip, but he just held tighter.

"Or how about the time you fucked my best friend? You were so high you couldn't tell the difference between me and him. That night you got treated like the hoe you were. Did you really think you could keep a secret like that from me, that you fucked for money?"

Monica started turning red, gasping for air. Eric released his grip, and she slid to the floor. Breathing heavily, Eric backed up and picked up his jacket that fell out his hands.

"If you hurt him, you're dead!" He said before leaving the condo.

****

Loyal sat in her car parked in front of Melissa's house. She finally let out all the emotions she was carrying. Her eyes were blood shot red for crying the entire way over there. When she opened her door, everything that she had consumed that night came up. Vomit splashed as she hunched over, leaning out of her car. Loyal felt a little better after bringing it all up, but she was still an emotional wreck.

All this time he's cheating on me, and he got the nerve to say I'm fucking with Kino. She thought to herself, trying to make sense of the situation. She felt the urge to throw up again, but this time wasn't able to open the door fast enough. Everything that was in her stomach was now either on her or the floor of her car. Miserable was and understatement. At times like this, she wished her mother was still living. She laid her head on the window and closed her eyes. She imagined her mother holding her and telling her everything was going to be okay. Loyal was thirteen when her mother died, and met Melissa shortly after. Melissa was a little older, and she was very over protective of Loyal. A single tear fell down Loyal's cheek.

How could I have been so naive?

Knock! Knock!

Loyal opened her eyes and saw Melissa standing there. She hadn't even heard a car pull up. Loyal opened the door and tried to get out of the car. Melissa saw the condition her best friend was in, and helped her into the house. No words were exchanged, but seeing Loyal in that state, Melissa felt bad for leaving her friend with no explanation.

"I can't do this anymore." Loyal said, letting out a loud cry.

Melissa could smell the alcohol coming from her pores. She had never known Loyal to drink this much. She took her best friend upstairs and cleaned her up. Soon after, Loyal was out of it, sound asleep like a newborn baby.

****

Kino beeped his horn when he reached his house. Meeka looked out the window and saw his car idling in the street. Smiling, she snatched up her bag, phone and keys, and headed out the door.

"Where are we going at 2 a.m.?" She said when she hopped in the passenger seat. "Our flight doesn't leave until eleven."

Kino didn't say a word. He kept his eyes on the road.

Meeka could see the disturbed look on his face. She felt something was wrong. She starting getting nervous but tried to remain cool just in case she was overreacting.

Putting her hand in her jacket pocket, she held on to her cell phone just in case she needed to get to it quickly.

Kino drove until they reached the Ben Franklin Bridge.

"Why are we going to New Jersey?" Meeka asked, still not getting any answers from Kino.

When they were clear across the bridge, Kino pulled to the side of the road and turned off the ignition. He looked Meeka in the eyes.

"What I'm about to ask you, I need an honest answer to." Kino started.

"What relation do you have with Trey?"

CHAPTER SIXTEEN

"I've never had so much fun in my life! I feel like I'm about to pass out." Angel said flopping onto the king-size hotel bed.

"I'm glad you enjoyed yourself." Pablo said, shutting the door behind him. He bought her to Atlantic City, New Jersey for a surprise dinner and a concert. They spent the rest of the evening on the blackjack table. It was Angel's first time playing black jack and her beginners luck must have kicked in because she was a beast on the table.

"Angel, come dance with me." Pablo said.

"Where's the music?"

"We don't need music." Pablo guided her off the bed. He took her in his arms and swayed side to side, slowly.

Angel let her body flow along with his and laid her head on his shoulder. There was no other place in the world that she would rather be.

"Why are you so good to me?" She asked. "You barely even know me, yet you're treating me as if I'm royalty."

"You're a good person, Angel. You deserve to be treated like so."

"Pablo, there is a lot you don't know about me."

"I know that you love me."

Angel lifted her head from his shoulder and looked in his eyes.

"You do love me, right?" Pablo asked when he saw the hesitant look on her face.

"Y-Y-Yes! Yes, I do." She said coming to the realization that she was really in love. It was the first time she'd ever told a man that she loved him. She lowered her head once more.

"And you know I love you as well?" Pablo asked. He lifted up her chin so that he could look in her eyes.

Angel nodded her head. Her eyes began to fill with tears. Pablo leaned in and kissed her, passionately. They both walked towards the bed still connected by the lips. Pablo laid her on the bed, kissing on her neck. She felt vibrating under her back and realized she was lying on her phone. She sat up to retrieve it. Meeka's name flashed across the screen. She sent the call the voicemail and turned off her phone.

"Who was that my love?" Pablo asked.

"No one important." Angel said, taking her shirt off and exposing her perky breast.

Pablo took one of her breast into his mouth.

There is no way her little ass is messing up my night. I will deal with her in the morning! Angel thought.

CHAPTER SEVENTEEN

Loyal woke up to the sound of *Deju Vu* by *Beyonce*. For a split second she almost had forgotten where she was. That ten hour rest was what she needed after such a chaotic night. She sat up in Melissa's bed and stretched her arms in the air. The pain she felt the night before still lingered in her heart. Too many thoughts were clouded mind making it hard to even start her day.

She climbed out of bed and opened the door. The smell of food rushing at her made her stomach growl.

"Mmm," Loyal moaned and headed down stairs to find her friend.

Melissa danced around the kitchen to the music with a spatula in one hand and a plate in the other.

"You feeling good this morning, huh?" Loyal said, startling her.

"I can't say the same for you," Melissa said, jokingly. "You need to leave that hard liquor to the big girls."

"Y'all big girls can have it all! I feel so crazy."